SPECIAL MESSAGE TO READERS

THE ULVERSCROFT FOUNDATION
(registered UK charity number 264873)

was established in 1972 to provide funds for research, diagnosis and treatment of eye diseases. Examples of major projects funded by the Ulverscroft Foundation are:-

- The Children's Eye Unit at Moorfields Eye Hospital, London
- The Ulverscroft Children's Eye Unit at Great Ormond Street Hospital for Sick Children
- Funding research into eye diseases and treatment at the Department of Ophthalmology, University of Leicester
- The Ulverscroft Vision Research Group, Institute of Child Health
- Twin operating theatres at the Western Ophthalmic Hospital, London
- The Chair of Ophthalmology at the Royal Australian College of Ophthalmologists

You can help further the work of the Foundation by making a donation or leaving a legacy. Every contribution is gratefully received. If you would like to help support the Foundation or require further information, please contact:

THE ULVERSCROFT FOUNDATION
The Green, Bradgate Road, Anstey
Leicester LE7 7FU, England
Tel: (0116) 236 4325

website: www.foundation.ulverscroft.com

TOO GOOD TO BE TRUE

The picturesque Canadian village of Pineville provides more than simple holiday relaxation when ex-journalist Amy Watson arrives to visit her relatives. What is she to do when she finds herself falling for hunky Luke, local businessman and environmentalist, when she will be flying back to the UK in just a few weeks? To make matters worse, Luke's beautiful and eminently fashionable fellow environmentalist Jill seems to be determined to win his heart first. Can Amy return to her old life, and leave Luke and Jill to each other?

Books by Wendy Kremer
in the Linford Romance Library:

WENDY KREMER

TOO GOOD TO BE TRUE

Complete and Unabridged

LINFORD
Leicester

First published in Great Britain in 2014

First Linford Edition
published 2015

A catalogue record for this book is available
from the British Library.

ISBN 978–1–4448–2624–1

Published by
F. A. Thorpe (Publishing)
Anstey, Leicestershire

Set by Words & Graphics Ltd.
Anstey, Leicestershire
Printed and bound in Great Britain by
T. J. International Ltd., Padstow, Cornwall

This book is printed on acid-free paper

1

Amy couldn't resist; she peered through the gaps in the lettering. Someone looked up and came to open the door. He had a pleasant face and a friendly smile and he invited her in with a sweeping motion. 'Ruth's, visitor I presume?'

Surprised, Amy hesitated. 'How do you . . . '

'Know? Ruth and Alan mentioned it last week. We go bowling together. Strangers are rare in Pineville. I'm Rod Taylor. This is Luke Thornton.'

A second man, sitting next to the desk, got up and held out his hand. His voice was friendly but his expression was guarded. 'Hi! Pleased to meet you.' For a moment he continued to measure her with his eyes.

She shook his hand briefly. His fingers were cool and smooth as they held hers. 'Hello.'

Rod pointed her towards a chair, and then sat down behind the desk.

She looked around, taking in the atmosphere while she explained. 'I'm between jobs at the moment. I've always wanted to visit Ruth. I thought this was the best chance I'd ever have.'

He nodded. 'Ruth told me you're a journalist.'

She smiled and tilted her head. 'I was one until a syndicate bought our newspaper, got rid of nearly everyone, and installed their own people. I've tried to find another job in journalism, without any luck, but I'm going to work for a publishing company at the end of October.'

'But you'd prefer to be in journalism, eh?'

She nodded. 'Um! Of course, but it hasn't worked out that way.'

'Reporting jobs aren't plentiful. Coffee?'

'Please.'

'Luke?'

Luke Thornton shook his head and got up. 'The packaging machine is blocked again. I'm meeting the plane to pick up some spare parts.'

Rod signalled his agreement. 'I'll see you later?'

'If we finish the repairs in time. About seven, otherwise I'll call, okay?' Luke Thornton addressed her politely. 'Bye, Miss . . . ?'

Amy liked his soft Canadian accent, noticed his steel-grey eyes and how his dark hair barely brushed the collar of his check flannel shirt. He was good to look at but gave her the impression he was more reserved than Rod. She obliged. 'Watson . . . Amy Watson.'

He gave her a curt nod, picked up his soft leather jacket, hooked it over his shoulder, and bent his head as he exited through the door.

Rod searched the general disorder on a side-table for a clean coffee mug. 'Milk? Sugar?'

'Milk if you've got any, please.'

'Only powdered, I'm afraid. Will that be okay?' She nodded. 'Tell me about your paper.' Rod studied her. Apart from some modest make-up, nothing about her looks came from the drugstore. Her auburn hair, creamy skin and hazel eyes were too well matched. He handed her some coffee and pushed a jar of instant milk in her direction.

Amy stirred in a spoonful and then circled the mug with her slender fingers. 'It was a local, like this one. Our town was bigger than Pineville, and the paper covered quite a large area. I was a junior reporter and just beginning to cover the more interesting stories. I loved it; no two days were the same.'

'I know what you mean. That's what I like too. That, and the fact that I'm occasionally able to influence opinion. Even locals here need stirring up sometimes.'

'How many people work here?'

'Joe's in charge of printing, Wally's our photographer and general factotum. And me.'

'Just you three? No chief editor or manager?'

4

He shrugged and grinned. 'I have to meet the board now and then. They ask questions and I forewarn them about anything special. They complain about costs, and raise hell about petty matters every time, but generally I have a free hand.'

'What about sales, advertising, marketing, et cetera?'

'Don't need them. People want to read about local news. They buy a regional or national if they're interested in wider topics. Most of them get their information about world affairs via the TV these days.'

Surprise echoed in her voice. 'And it pays its way?'

He gave her a wry grin. 'Circulation is steady and it makes a slight profit. I've thought about how I could modernise it, make it more snazzy and upbeat, but the owners won't take a gamble, so everything stays roughly as it is. They may be right. People might like it, but then again not. Folks hereabouts are pretty conservative.'

'You don't mind or get frustrated?'

'No.' He smiled infectiously. 'I still enjoy making it as attention-grabbing as I can. Most people don't notice, but I'm changing things gradually anyway. Whenever I asked if I should modernise something, they said, 'Leave it alone boy, we like it as it is!' I wait a while and then do it anyway. I wouldn't have the freedom that I have here anywhere else.'

'I'm impressed that you produce it with so few people.'

'We pitch out ten to twelve sides every week with the help of computers, and because the three of us are a good team. Some weeks lots happens, other times hardly anything at all. That's when I fall back on the middle-of-the-road stuff that's not too outdated. I keep a drawer full and I'm always on the lookout for more for filling the gaps.'

Amy took a sip of coffee. 'It sounds great.'

'It is, but I remind myself constantly

I am not allowed to take sides, because there's no one around to tell me to slam on the brakes and be impartial. It's an uphill fight and when we go to print it's chaotic.' His pale blue eyes twinkled.

She liked him. Taking a sip of coffee — it was strong and tasted bitter — she asked, 'Who owns it? The man who was just here — Luke?'

Body forward and with his head slightly tilted, Rod ran his fingers through his hair; some disobedient yellow strands flopped back onto his forehead. 'What makes you think that?'

She shrugged. 'I don't know. Just an assumption.'

'I think he owns some of the shares, but he doesn't come to meetings unless I ask him to. As far as I know, the *Gazette* belongs to the bank and a handful of other local businessmen like Luke.'

She couldn't stop herself. 'What does he do?'

'Luke? Oh, he runs two small firms in Pineville.' Her expression remained curious, so he continued. 'Luke planned to remain in Vancouver after university. His mother had a long-lasting illness, and during his visits he noticed how things were going downhill locally. He astonished everyone when he came back and set up the companies. The one makes electronic parts for other firms, and the second one repairs engines and generators. They seem to be very successful. These days the city authorities have wheedled him into helping out with the planning and organization of winter tourism around here. If it takes off, that might trigger summer tourism as well.'

Amy wanted to ask more, but she resisted. 'Were you born here?'

'No. I moved to Pineville three years ago. I come from Ottawa.'

'Married?'

'No, but I'm ready to change that, as soon as I find the right woman!' Rod grinned and looked pointedly at her left hand. 'What about you? No husband, no steady boyfriend or fiancé?'

Amy broke into an open, friendly

smile. 'No, no one special. You know what a reporter's life is like — irregular hours, overtime, et cetera. After a while my boyfriends found it hard to accept that.'

Amy thought briefly about her last boyfriend. How he'd disliked the week-end assignments and occasional overtime. He'd retaliated by cheating on her. A colleague had seen him and put her in the picture. When she confronted him, they'd quarrelled about her work and his cheating. She finally realized just how unsuited they were. After the initial upset, she realized she didn't like him as much as she thought she had, but her pride was hurt. She'd vowed not to get involved again unless she loved the person passionately and was sure he accepted her, and what she did, without a qualm. She'd now lost her job and also begun to wonder if she'd ever find anyone to love.

'Ah!' Rod gave her a speculative look. 'So, you're a career woman?'

'In a way, but I hope that I'm not the

cut-throat kind who excludes any other options. I'd like a husband and family one day, with the right person. I'm giving my job priority at present, and leaving the rest to fate.'

'Female reporters often have a hard time. It's a pretty demanding profession for a woman, especially when she has a family.'

She shrugged. 'All journalistic work is demanding. It shouldn't be more demanding for a woman than a man. It starts to fall apart when there's a family to look after and everyone assumes that it's solely the woman's responsibility.' She hooked her hair behind her ear. 'A female reporter needs someone who shares the domestic problems without a quibble. Small newspapers don't make such big demands. A major paper expects one hundred and fifty percent. That's where you need professional help, and that costs money. I'm not worrying about it at the moment; perhaps I'll stay single. Perhaps I'll never find another job in journalism.'

She looked thoughtful. 'Can I call, to see you put the paper to bed?'

'Sure thing! It all comes together on Thursday afternoon. The paper goes on sale on Friday morning. Come whenever you like. You'll meet Joe and Wally.' He paused. 'Perhaps you'd enjoy coming on an interview with me one day? And you can give us an article on a visitor's impressions of Pineville.'

'I'd love to, although I'll need to know Pineville better to write about it. Sure that I won't get in the way?'

He shook his head firmly. 'I'll plonk you in the corner and you can check the proofs, or I'll find you something else to do. How long are you staying?'

'Until September, or the beginning of October if I like it here.'

He whistled softly. 'That's a long vacation. I hope you won't get bored; this is a quiet place.'

'I won't! I'm an enthusiastic reader. I'm looking forward to relaxing and doing some sight-seeing.'

'We're not exactly a focal point of

Canadian tourism around here yet, but it's great countryside. If you like reading, our local library is well stocked. Perhaps we can take in a movie one evening?'

'Perhaps.' She looked down at her watch. 'Ruth will wonder where I am. Thanks for the coffee.' She smiled and got up.

He eyed her slim figure admiringly as she zipped her anorak. 'My pleasure!'

He followed her out. Once Amy was on the other side of the road, she turned to check. Rod was still standing in the doorway watching her, and she waved.

As she strolled homewards, her eyes were drawn to the soaring mountains surrounding the small town. Pineville nestled in the bowl of the valley, and the spontaneous greetings of the people she passed showed her it was a friendly place. Taking a deep breath of crystal-clear air, she studied the towering pinnacles shrouded in drifts of swirling grey-and-white clouds. There were deep bluish-purple splashes high up in the peaks, between smidgens of white where the snow and ice still persisted. Firs, in shades of rich green, fought for a foothold among the grey rocks and they flourished thickly along the lower slopes.

Amy thrust her hands into her pockets and hurried home to her mother's cousin. She hung up her jacket in the narrow hallway and went to the kitchen.

Ruth was ironing. 'Hi! So . . . what do you think?'

'I like it. People are welcoming and the scenery is breathtaking.'

The smell of freshly laundered clothes filled the air as Ruth's busy hands travelled back and forth. 'When you live here, you take the scenery for granted. How about some tea and muffins?'

'I'll skip the tea, but a muffin sounds good. I've just had coffee with Rod at the newspaper office. I was curious, looked in and . . . '

Ruth's face creased into a smile.

'Rod? He's a nice guy.'

'I've invited myself back to see how the paper is put together.'

'Of course, I expect you'd enjoy that.' The iron continued to make smooth inroads into one of Alan's shirts.

Amy switched on the kettle and took a chocolate muffin from a plate. Munching contentedly, she mumbled, 'I met someone else there. Luke Thornton.'

'Luke?'

'Know him?'

'Sure! This is a small place; everyone knows everyone else. He's Alan's boss.'

'He didn't stay long.'

'Luke's a clever chap. He's not as outgoing as Rod, but he's just as nice when you get to know him properly. He's made his mark, and is very popular in the town. He created new jobs when things were going downhill fast.'

'So I heard. A captain of industry, eh?' She brushed some crumbs from the corner of her mouth with the tip of her finger.

'I don't know if that's the right

14

description, but he's smart. Alan was out of work for six months until Luke opened the electronics factory.'

Amy nodded. 'What about Luke's wife? Does she visit the poor and needy, and distribute presents and food at Christmas?' Amy tilted her head and her eyes sparkled mischievously.

Ruth smiled. 'Oh, go on with you! This is not Britain in the Middle Ages. We don't have a lord of the manor. Luke's okay. He's not married, although there are plenty of girls around here who'd like to change that if they could.'

Amy shrugged. 'He sounds like he's too good to be true. Can I have another muffin?'

2

Ruth's husband Alan whistled as he came down the hallway a couple of hours later. He kissed Ruth, ruffled Amy's rusty hair, and threw himself into a chair, then looked at Amy. 'I'll have to fight to keep the single guys out when the word gets round.'

Amy chuckled and her hair bounced around her face. 'Then local men must be desperate.'

He watched her indulgently. 'Just wait and see! Phoned your mom?'

'This morning, just to reassure her that I'd arrived safely.'

He nodded. 'Good! How about food, Ruthie? I'm starving.'

Ruth's blue eyes twinkled and she eyed him fondly. 'You always are. Beef casserole, mushrooms and dumplings. It's almost ready!'

During the meal, Amy and Ruth

talked about relatives and friends back home. Alan leaned back listening. Waiting for a break in the conversation, he said, 'Tonight is choir practice. Come with us. It'll give you a chance to meet some other people.'

Amy jettisoned her idea about an early night.

★ ★ ★

The local community hall was on the other side of the town; it was a simple wooden construction. Inside, rows of chairs faced a raised platform. Like lots of rooms that are seldom used, it had slight traces of neglect and a whiff of mustiness. Ruth introduced Amy to various people. She heard all about British relatives or where families had originally come from. After the choir-master arrived, Amy sat on a stiff chair among the shadows and listened. They sang with gusto, clearly enjoying them-selves. During the pause Amy decided to offer to help, mainly to get away from any more questions.

Ruth pointed her towards the kitchen. 'Judy organises things, and she's always grateful for help.'

A tall young woman with black hair and grey eyes was busy at the sink. She was obviously pregnant. 'Can I help?' Amy asked her.

She looked up and smiled. 'Gladly! Will you pour the milk?'

They were busy for a while and there was little chance for conversation. People came to collect their coffee and then things quietened again. Judy smiled at Amy. 'That's the first rush, but they'll be back again for seconds in a couple of minutes. Who are you?' She handed Amy a cup of coffee and Amy helped herself to milk.

'Amy, Amy Watson.'

'Ah! Ruth's visitor. My brother said he'd met you this morning at the newspaper office.'

Amy hesitated and then asked, 'You're Rod's sister?'

She laughed. 'Rod? Good heavens,

no. I'm Judy Harrison, Luke's sister.'

'Oh, yes — now I see the resemblance.'

'You're on vacation?'

'Yes, for a couple of weeks.'

She nodded. 'The town doesn't get many tourists, but we hope that the new ski lift may change all that. It's very quiet here most of the time.'

A smile tipped the corners of Amy's mouth. 'Rod told me about those plans this morning. Are you a working wife, a housewife, or a mixture of both?'

Judy smiled. 'I've just finished teaching at the local junior school.' She patted her rounded middle. 'Don and I already have a little boy. Tim is nearly four. We decided I'd take a break until Tim is in school and this next one is in kindergarten.' She gave a small sigh. 'The Canadian government supports working mothers better than many other countries, but it still means a lot of organising if you opt for children and a career.'

Amy nodded. 'I expect it's never easy.

19

Women in general have a hard time of co-ordinating it all. You want to go back to teaching later?'

Judy straightened her shoulders unconsciously and said confidently, 'Of course! My husband Don is very supportive. I can't imagine not ever teaching again, even if we had bags of money, which we don't.' Her eyes twinkled.

'When's your baby due?'

'In five weeks — no, less than that now. Four and a half.' She smiled. 'I'll miss my class. What about you? Married? Children?'

'Not married, and no children. I'm an ex-reporter, between jobs. I'm starting new work in October, so it's an ideal time for me to visit Ruth. I've wanted to for years, but somehow something else always got in the way.'

'Come and visit me one afternoon. When Tim finds out you're English, he'll do a somersault. For some reason, at present he's fixed on soldiers, especially ones with fancy uniforms.'

Amy's brow wrinkled. 'Then I'm

afraid I'll be a huge disappointment. I don't know anything about the British army.'

'Don't worry, neither does he. My father-in-law seems to have wakened his interest.' She smiled. 'Do call.'

'Are you sure?'

'Very. I love company. I'm still getting used to not having to go to work every day! How about Monday? Or have you something else planned?'

Amy shook her head. 'Where do you live?'

'Know your way around?'

'Not very well. I only arrived yesterday.'

'Know the disused station buildings where the railway track peters out — near the fire station, on the edge of town?'

'I noticed the fire station when I arrived.'

'Cross the tracks and go up the sloping road opposite. Our homestead is on the bend of the road. The only other place is Luke's, and that's round

21

the next bend, so you can't go wrong.'

'What time?'

'Any time. Come whenever you feel like it, after lunch.'

People rushed in for more coffee. When the singing began again, Amy told Judy to join the others. She could manage to load and unpack the industrial dishwasher on her own. Judy smiled and left. Amy was grateful for her spontaneous friendliness.

* * *

After a day or two, Amy had adjusted to the feeling of freedom. It didn't take her long to find her way around Pineville; it was a small place. She sometimes pushed a book into her pocket and went to sit on the silent slopes overlooking the town, among the quiet and beauty of the sun-drenched scenery. As she climbed the slopes, her feet sunk into layers of hard dried grass, bracken and brown pine needles that whispered under her sensible shoes.

There was a strong smell of resin and pine in the air. Ever since her arrival the weather had been fantastic; the sky was cobalt-blue with drifting wisps of white clouds.

Rod phoned her at the end of the week and invited her to come on an interview. A gas-station owner had been robbed the previous night. It was interesting to watch how Rod handled the interview, and how he reported it in the next edition. Pineville might not be at the centre of the world, but they had a good reporter. On their way back from the interview, Amy asked him if he knew where she could buy something for a little boy who was interested in soldiers.

He scratched the back of his head for a moment. 'Hm! I'm not sure, but I've got a good idea where we can try. We'll visit Ernie. He has a barn stuffed to the rafters with books, and all sorts of other things.'

★　★　★

Amy found Judy's home easily on Monday afternoon. The sprawling log cabin nestled in a green hollow set back from the road. The area around the house was clear of trees, but the forest rippled a dark emerald green in the background and there was a bright flowerbed in front of the long veranda. Judy came out to greet her, holding her son's hand.

'Hi! Glad you made it. This is Tim.' Judy looked fresh and cool; her thick dark hair was pinned back behind her ears, and she wore a voluminous white blouse over red cotton pants.

Amy squatted down in front of the little boy and handed him a book. 'Hello, Tim! I've heard that you like soldiers. I've brought a book about them; I hope you'll like it.'

Amy could tell he would. His blue eyes lit up instantly. He smiled at his mother and without prompting, murmured quietly 'Thank you' before he darted off into the house with it clutched firmly to his chest.

'Good heavens! Where did you find that?' Judy said.

'I was in Sandville last Friday with Rod. He knew a man who had a lot of second-hand stuff. Among other things, there were hundreds, if not thousands, of books. Amazingly, the owner knew where to put his hand on everything. The book smells a bit musty. I hope you don't mind that it's not new.'

'Of course not. That was probably Ernie Booth's place. It's not easy to get any specialist books around here. You have to order stuff online or have it sent from one of the bigger towns. Specialist books are always expensive. Trust Rod to know where to find something. It was kind of you to think of Tim. Do you want tea or coffee?'

'I really don't mind. I hope you haven't gone to any extra trouble.'

'No, I bought the cake. Sit down, Amy.' She pointed her towards a chair on the veranda and disappeared into the house. The small table was laid with crisp white mats and delicate china. In the centre was a clear glass vase with a handful of bright red poppies, moving gently in the breeze. More than anything else, Amy was aware of the silence.

Tim came back and positioned himself next to Amy. Curiosity had overcome his shyness. 'Do you know which one's a Coldstream Guard?' He began to turn the pages. Amy read the captions and she found him the desired picture. He beamed.

When Judy came back, she chortled. 'Oh dear! Let Amy and Mom have tea now, please. Want something to drink?'

He shook his head, picked up the book and went indoors.

'He's adorable. He's very polite and intelligent!' Amy hooked the teacup and began to sip her tea. She was thirsty.

'Yes, he's a good kid.' Judy couldn't keep the pride out of her voice. 'Don thinks he's a genius and Luke spoils him. I have to watch they don't overstep the mark.'

'Our next-door neighbour has a

four-year-old and he throws tantrums every single day. He's found out that if he protests loud enough, his parents give in. Tim is an angel in comparison.'

'I can see he's made another conquest.' Judy smiled. 'You like children?'

'I have a two-year-old nephew, but unfortunately we don't see him very often,' Amy explained. 'My brother and his family live in London. I haven't very much experience of children, but from what I've seen of them I like them very much.'

'I've always loved children. I have them around me all the time when I teach and now I've almost got two in my private life.'

The conversation flowed freely. Judy said she was a member of the local historical society and she told Amy about the town's history. 'We have a small museum. A group of us set it up last year and asked people to contribute items. We had a good response and we now have lots of memorabilia.'

'It sounds interesting. I'll call one day.'

'Do! It's not ancient history compared to what you have in England, but anything older than a couple of centuries is old here. We're also trying to find items of local indigenous peoples to exhibit, but that's proving more difficult.'

'And you sit there, waiting for visitors?'

'Yep! One afternoon a week, in summer. Two friends take the other two days. We don't get many visitors, but we live in hope. We close in winter, but if winter tourism takes off, we'll probably open then too. We'll need to offer other attractions apart from the movies, the local sports centre and various community activities. Pineville is a quiet place.'

'When are you there?'

'Every Tuesday, until the end of October. I usually take Tim with me.'

Amy looked out across the silent meadow towards the forest. There was a mass of bushes with bluish-green colour spread out along the fringes. Amy and Judy continued to chat and Tim reappeared with the book. His head shot up when he heard a jeep coming down the gravel track. Abandoning the book, he clambered down the steps on chubby legs to meet his father, and chortled as he was thrown up into the air.

Tim was still clinging to his father when Don Harrison bent to kiss his wife. He was a strong, muscular man, soft-spoken, with a delightful Canadian drawl. He and Tim had the same colouring. He shook Amy's hand politely and gave her a broad smile. 'Hi there! I've heard all about you. News travels fast in this place.' He sighed contentedly and sank into a chair. Tim promptly clambered up onto his knee, clutching the book again.

Judy looked pointedly at Amy and winked. 'Like some more tea, Amy?'

Amy stood up. 'No, thanks. It was great to see you again and to meet the family, but I'll be off now.'

'I hope to see you again soon. At the museum perhaps?'

'Yes, I'll call — promise. Bye, Don! Bye, Tim!'

Don looked up. 'Hope I'm not chasing you away?'

Amy smiled at him. 'No, I've been here ages already.'

Judy came with her to the steps. Looking towards the road, Amy saw Luke Thornton coming towards the house with a slender blonde woman at his side. Judy saw them too. She gave an involuntary explanation. 'Oh! Luke mentioned he wanted to introduce us to someone who works for an environmental organisation. Apparently her job is to check existing, or former, trouble spots so that they can decide about any necessary action. She's visiting our area at present. Luke's always been passionate about environmental protection. Someone told her he was the right person to help her around here, and she got in touch with him. Stay and meet them.'

Amy shook her head. 'I won't, if you don't mind. I promised Ruth and Alan I'd cook the evening meal today and I'm already behind schedule. Another time perhaps.'

'Then I'll look forward to seeing you at the museum.'

'Yes. Till Tuesday!'

The woman was good-looking, slim and blonde. She was a perfect foil to Luke's tall, dark looks. Amy didn't understand why she felt a mite irritated. Perhaps it was the way the other woman eyed her clothes and figure with a hint of condescension. She smiled at Amy, but the smile never reached her eyes.

Luke's expression was bland. 'Hi! A surprise to see you here.' His black hair gleamed in the sunshine.

She locked her hands behind her back. 'I met Judy at choir practice and she invited me.'

He nodded and turned to his companion. 'This is Jill Edwards. She's another visitor to Pineville. She works

31

for Ecosystems Canada. Jill, this is Amy, Amy Watson. She's a visitor from the UK.'

Amy shoved her misgivings aside. 'Hi! Judy just explained that you're checking the surrounding area for trouble spots.'

Jill was above average height. Her flax-coloured trouser suit skimmed her willowy figure. Her fingers played with a cream silk scarf looped loosely round her neck. 'Yes, we inspect endangered spots, settle disputes, help solve problems, or set legal machinery in motion to force owners to clear up the mess or the damage. Luke knows all the weak spots locally and his information will save me a lot of time and trouble. You're on vacation? How long are you staying? Pineville is an interesting little town, with some very agreeable attractions, isn't it?'

Amy wondered if she was subtly inferring to Luke Thornton. Looking at him now, Amy decided it was understandable. He still had an air of reservation, so if Jill was interested in him in a special way, she might find he wasn't a pushover. She shook her wandering thoughts and stuck her hand into her pocket. 'I'm here for a couple of weeks, just visiting relatives. It was nice to meet you. Good luck with the work. Judy's husband just got home. I think they're waiting for you on the veranda. Bye!' She gave them both a stilted nod and wished the colour didn't suddenly cover her cheeks when she met Luke's eyes. How silly of her!

Jill managed a halting 'Cheerio' before she turned away towards the homestead.

Amy turned away abruptly and Luke watched the English girl in her jeans and checked blouse for a moment before he hurried to catch up with Jill, who'd almost reached the veranda steps.

3

The museum was a former family home. It had a tinny-sounding, tinkling bell above the door. Judy sat behind a rough-hewn table reading a book. She looked up and smiled.

'Amy, how nice! A visitor at last.'

'Not a busy day then?' Amy answered.

Judy had an endearing habit of tilting her head. 'No. Tim! Come and see who's here.' Tim appeared and trotted confidently towards Amy.

'Hi, Tim! What are you doing?'

'Playing cars.' He handed her a crimson sports car.

Amy examined it. 'Gosh, what an eye-catcher.' She ruffled his hair and gave it back.

Judy said, 'Go on, take a look around. I'll make us some coffee.'

'Will you show me around, Tim?' Amy held out her hand. His face brightened and he shoved his hand confidently into hers. They went from room to room and his squeaky voice repeated what he'd picked up from adults about various items he thought were interesting. They lingered longer in the children's bedroom, examining the old-fashioned toys, before finally coming back downstairs to Judy. She was seated in the former parlour. Tim drank some juice and then wandered off to find his abandoned car.

Amy said offhandedly, 'It's very interesting. I'm surprised that people have kept so much old . . . stuff.' Her voice trailed off lamely.

'Don't you dare! You were about to say rubbish, weren't you?' Judy laughed throatily. 'Just wait, one day they'll be bona fide antiques. We hope it will show how ordinary people lived when they first came here. Kitchens were places of drudgery, bedrooms weren't cosy boudoirs, and living rooms were draughty and dusty. Life was very hard back then.'

Loose tendrils framed Amy's face. She nodded. 'I'm not nitpicking, honestly; in fact it's very interesting. I'm just surprised that so many ugly, unwieldy everyday items have survived. Some of the kitchen equipment looks like instruments of torture.'

'Ah, well! Pineville was very isolated and cut off. People couldn't afford to buy everything even if they had the chance to get it. They sometimes pinched the design and idea and copied as best they could. The result was often effective, but primitive in appearance. What they'd bought or made, they kept, even though no one used it anymore.'

'Is there an entrance fee?'

'No. We raffle a quilt once a year, to help cover the overheads.'

'How much?'

'A dollar a ticket.'

'Okay. Give me five.'

Amy shoved them into her bag and Judy wrote her name on the stubs. She asked, 'What've you done since we last met?'

'Not much. I read a lot, wander around, and on Ruth's working days I do the cooking. Alan lets me use his jeep if he doesn't need it and I drive around admiring the scenery. The towns are so far apart! I'm afraid of leaving the main road, in case I get lost. I'm used to villages and towns being fairly close to each other. But I like it here. I want to visit Vancouver for a couple of days before I leave. How are you feeling?'

'Like an elephant. I'd love to get some more exercise but I promised Don not to go off on my own.' She eyed Amy hopefully. 'Have you been up to the Look Out yet?'

'No. Ruth mentioned it. Where is it and what is it?'

'Just a viewpoint. It's between here and the next town, at the top of the hill. I'd like to take you there. What about it? Don can't object if you're with me. I've a clinic check-up tomorrow. How about Thursday? I'm sure Luke will take Tim for a couple of hours if I ask him. He works at home some days if he's not needed in the office.'

'If you're sure it's not risky for you, I'm game. Where do we meet, what time?'

'There's a path that begins at the far end of the CV Park. It leads there. Know where to find the campground? Not many folks stop here on their way east or west, but in the summer it's busier. We hope it will be a lot busier if the tourism plans take off.'

Amy nodded. 'Yes, I know where the campground is. I've seen the sign on the road.'

'The path up to and past the Look Out is a short-cut to Burkedom. Nowadays most people go by car around the foot of the mountain. When we get to the top, we can come back another way and finish up at the rear of our homestead. How about four o'clock?' Amy nodded and Judy added, 'Have you seen any bears since you came?'

'Bears?' Amy spluttered. 'No, thank heavens!'

Judy laughed. 'They inhabit the forest all round here. We rarely see one in town in the summer, but in winter they sometimes sneak in to raid the trash bins, mostly at night.'

'Then I'm glad I'm here now and not in the winter. What if I meet one? I've been relaxing out on the slopes around the town. I didn't give a second thought to bears or any other animals.'

Judy tipped her head. Her eyes twinkled. 'If I were you, I'd just tell them that foreign fare doesn't taste very good.'

Amy's eyes widened. 'Judy, that's not funny. The only place I've ever seen a bear is on TV.'

Judy smiled at Amy's nervous expression. 'Don't worry! You're not likely to meet any. Just don't panic if you do. Keep quiet and stand still. They won't normally attack unless they feel threatened. They try to avoid humans, so make a noise when you walk through the forests. You do have to be very careful if they have cubs though.' She pushed a chair in Amy's direction. 'Sit down and tell me about your home and your work.'

They chatted. Judy talked about her work, too, and she could tell that Judy was already missing her job. Time passed quickly. Amy looked at her watch. 'It's almost closing time, isn't it? I'll see you Thursday then?' Judy nodded.

Amy shouldered her bag, headed for the door, and shouted as she went, 'Bye Tim!' Tim hurried into the room and waved her off.

She was back on Main Street in a matter of minutes. Someone sounded the horn when he passed, and she looked up. It was Luke. Amy doubted that he'd seen her wave back. She'd reacted too sluggishly.

He had, though. Luke glanced in his rear-view mirror at her slim figure walking with easy strides along the wooden planking. He continued to eye her until his car rounded the bend and she was finally lost to his sight.

Amy decided to call at the newspaper office on the way. Rod looked up when she came in. 'Hi! I'm going on another interview tomorrow. Want to come?'

Amy felt nostalgic when she smelt the printing ink. 'If you're sure I won't get in the way. What's it about?'

'A centenarian's birthday celebration; readers love that kind of thing.'

'Won't they mind you including me in the visit?'

'No, this woman lives with her daughter's family and loves being the centre of attention. What have you been doing?'

'I've just come from Pineville's local museum.'

'Wow! That'll be a holiday experience to remember.' He smiled broadly.

'Don't be so demeaning. It was interesting. It's really surprising what has survived.' She played with the papers on his desk. 'Shall I meet you here, at the office?'

'No, I'll pick you up; nine-thirty?'

'Okay. Do you still want an article from me about how a visitor sees Pineville?'

He nodded. 'Of course.'

'I still need to find out more about the town's history before I put pen to paper. How many words do you want?'

'Try the local library for historical facts. Anything up to two thousand words would be great.'

'Perhaps I can offer you something for next week's issue or the one after that.'

* * *

Next morning, he picked her up and Amy decided her initial impression about him lingered. Rod was uncomplicated and he had a delightful sense of humour. She enjoyed his company. He was easygoing, but took his work seriously. The centenarian was a lively interview partner. She'd come to Canada with her parents as a baby. It was amazing to hear her talking about past events.

When they got back to town, Amy adjusted her shoulder bag, ready to get out.

Rod asked, 'What about a movie tonight? It's the latest Brad Pitt.'

She liked him. 'Why not? What time?'

'Seven? We'll go to the Blue Boar for a beer after.'

'Okay. I'll meet you outside the cinema.'

'Right, outside the movie house.'

Amy laughed. 'Okay, outside the movie house, at seven.'

When they visited the Blue Boar after the movie, conversation stopped for a second. Everyone knew everyone else in Pineville and several men fired wise-cracks at Rod as they threaded their way to an empty table. Daylight was fading fast, and the light from the green cone-shaped shades threw golden circles onto the wooden surface.

They drank cold beers and talked about the movie, work, and things in general. He walked her home and she stuck out her hand. 'Thanks, Rod.'

He took it, and then kissed her cheek. It was an innocent gesture but Amy didn't want to encourage him. She wasn't looking for a holiday romance or a quick affair. If Rod asked her out again, she'd make that clear.

He smiled. 'Bring me your article in whenever you're ready. We must do this again real soon.'

Amy nodded. 'Perhaps!'

4

It was a beautiful afternoon when Amy set out to meet Judy. She was waiting, sitting on the crossbar of a fence, her legs at an angle to make it more comfortable to take the swell of her stomach. She got down when she spotted Amy and they walked towards the path. Judy pointed out various places in Pineville as they climbed the steep track upwards. Gradually the town was spread out below them. Amy plodded alongside and noticed that in comparison to Judy, she wasn't very fit. She breathed heavily and said, 'Gosh, this is more demanding than I expected. How do you feel?'

'I'm fine. If you want a rest, just say so.'

She shook her head. If a pregnant woman could stride up the hill easily, so could she. When they reached the crest and she'd caught her breath again, Amy saw it was worth the effort. It was still a bright summer day, full of sunlight, and Amy took several photos of the surrounding countryside, and of Judy, and Judy and her together. 'I'll send you copies when I'm home.'

They sat for a while, gossiping. Judy told her a little about Burkedom huddling among the fir trees down below them on the other side. Her interest in, and knowledge of, local history was obvious. They went back via another barely visible path winding down through the forest on the other side of the path. It was steeper, but they were both careful. Eventually, the path levelled out and branched to the left and the right. Judy preceded her along the right trail and eventually they emerged behind Judy's cabin. They paused for a moment.

Amy commented, 'I enjoyed that, even if I'm not in top form.'

Judy smiled. 'Good! When the kids are older, Don and I intend to go camping again. We often did so before Tim was born. Since then, we've let things slip a bit because you have to take so much more with you when you have a baby with you. We go out to the family cabin by the lake now and then, but that's not really camping.'

Amy had her hands on her hips. 'I've never been on a real camping expedition. The nearest I've got is when my dad put up a tent for us on our back lawn in the summer. If I went into any of your forests I'd get lost in no time.'

Judy nodded. 'Probably. You need to use the sun or the stars to keep you on course. Nowadays people who go into the wilds have handheld GPS systems. They eliminate the work as long as they connect reliably to a satellite.'

'Did you never want to live anywhere else?'

'I loved training in Vancouver, but Pineville is where I belong.'

They walked through the fragrant grass to the cabin. Judy unlocked the door and fresh mountain air invaded the silent rooms. Judy said, 'I need to go to the bathroom. The kitchen is the first on the left. Get us some fruit juice from the icebox. Glasses are in the cupboard by the window.'

Amy put the things on a tray in Judy's tidy kitchen and returned to the living room. She browsed through a glossy magazine lying on the table until she heard Judy calling. Amy found her sitting on the bed in the main bedroom.

'Don't panic, and you won't have to act as midwife, but the baby's started.' She saw Amy's startled expression.

Amy felt guilty. 'Perhaps the walk was too much for you?'

Judy shook her head. 'It's nothing to do with that. The clinic told me it could arrive any day.' She breathed deeply. 'Don's company has a special order on the go. He said he'd be late today. I've tried to call him but no luck; I expect he's forgotten to recharge his phone. With our first baby Tim took over twelve hours to arrive once my waters broke; second babies are usually faster.

Luke ignores his phone when he's working, but he's at home with Tim. Will you go there and explain, and take care of Tim until Don comes? I think I won't hang around here too long. I don't know when Don will turn up. I'd rather go to the hospital now.'

Amy tried to sound unperturbed. 'Of course; it's no problem. What about packing a suitcase?'

'My bag's ready.'

'Will you be all right until I get Luke?'

Judy smiled and pulled a face as the next contraction came. 'Ouch! Oh! I didn't expect the next one so soon.' She looked at Amy's nervous expression. 'Nothing's going to happen for a while yet. Don't worry. You can't miss Luke's place; it's up the road, round the next bend. Off you go.'

Amy nodded and left. She walked unhurried until she was out of sight of the cabin, then as soon as she reached the winding road she began to run. Around the bend, she soon saw another cabin. There was a white fence around the property and the gateway was open. She was out of breath and barely registered her surroundings as she left the road and sprinted up the gravelled pathway across the open grassland towards the cabin. His jeep was parked in an open carport next to another car. She took the veranda steps on the run and her footsteps echoed on the planking. The front door was open and she hurried inside without knocking. She could hear Tim's high-pitched voice and followed the sound down a corridor leading out of the living room.

Luke looked startled as she burst in. The sleeves of his cotton shirt were rolled up to his elbows and expensive-looking jeans clung to slim hips. A frown deepened above his jet-black brows. 'Hi, Amy. Something wrong? I thought you were out walking with Judy?'

Amy was still out of breath. She looked pointedly from him to Tim and back. She was glad when Luke reacted as she hoped. 'Tim, will you get Amy a can of 7-Up from the ice-box, please?'

'Hi, Tim!' She smiled and winked at him.

Luke waited until Tim was out of hearing, and then he asked, 'Is it the baby?'

She nodded. 'Judy wants you to take her to the hospital.'

His face clouded and his mouth tightened. 'It's too early, isn't it?'

She shrugged. 'Judy isn't worried. Don's on a special contract job and she can't reach him via his phone. She thinks it's best to go to hospital straight away, just in case.'

He glanced at his watch and she waited. His indecision fading fast, he switched off the computer and looked down at the papers spread over the desk. He left them, got up, and grabbed his jacket from the back of the chair while explaining, 'I was just checking and printing out the particulars about known trouble spots locally for Jill. You met her once, didn't you?'

Amy nodded. 'Judy asked me to stay with Tim. I'll walk home with him after

51

you've left. He might get upset if we come back with you now, and he sees Judy going.'

He nodded absentmindedly, while running his long fingers through his black hair. 'Thanks. The door will fall into the lock when you leave.'

'Remember to leave Judy's door open when you leave there.' She felt an urge to reassure him. 'Don't worry; apparently the clinic told Judy they thought the baby might arrive any day. Judy seems unconcerned and that's a good sign. Wish her all the best from me.'

He looked at her; his slate-grey eyes were guarded. They exchanged a polite smile of mutual encouragement before he went. Amy heard the wheels of his car spin as he raced off.

Tim came back carrying a misted can of 7-Up. 'That looks wonderful.' She pulled the tab and it zished. She took a gulp of cold liquid.

Tim smiled and looked around for Luke. He was expecting some words of praise. 'Where's Uncle Luke?'

'He's taking your mom to hospital. Your new brother or sister is about to be born.'

He looked at her, mouth slightly open, his face lit up with excitement.

'Will you let me look after you until Daddy comes home from work?' He nodded. 'Good.' She looked at his toys on the floor. 'Want to take anything with you?' His eyes were still bright.

'No, only Humphrey.'

Amy blessed providence that he was such an uncomplicated character. 'Who's Humphrey?'

'My blue rabbit, over there. All the other things live with Uncle Luke.'

Together they collected the scattered toys and put them into a big wooden box in the corner. Tim danced down the corridor, while Amy followed him and hurried to catch up.

'Did you have a coat, Tim?' He shook his head.

The afternoon sun was still warm. Amy pulled the door and it closed with an audible click. She reached for Tim's hand. He hung on to his rabbit with the other hand, dragging it along the floor, and chatting quite happily. Amy asked him about the blue soft toy's life history.

When they reached Judy's the door was open, and Tim ran straight in. He stopped suddenly as he began to absorb reality. Amy tried to distract him. 'Hey! I'd like to see that book about the soldiers again, before your dad arrives.'

He rushed off and clambered up next to Amy on the settee. They were almost finished talking about the various uniforms in detail by the time Don came in. He whistled cheerfully and noticed her with Tim. 'Hi, Amy. Where's Mom, Tim?'

Tim said, 'She's gone to hospital.'

Don's face froze. He looked at Amy. She nodded. 'Tim, I think it would be a good idea if Dad goes to check that your mom's okay.'

'I want to go with him too.' He looked confused; his lips began to quiver.

Don sought to reassure him. 'I'll

come back as soon as I can, Timmy. There's nothing for you to play with at the hospital; you'd get bored.'

Tim's lower lip jutted rebelliously. Amy wondered if he'd burst into tears. She was relieved when his pouting expression cleared and he asked, 'If I stay here, will Amy read Pooh Bear to me?'

Amy said, 'Of course I will, from back to front if you like.

Timmy still looked a little mulish but he was pacified for the moment.

'Be a pal, put my lunch box in the kitchen, there's a good boy.' Don handed him the plastic container, and Tim ran off. Then he turned to Amy.

She explained. 'Luke took her to the hospital.'

'But the baby's not due yet for a couple of weeks.'

How was she supposed to reassure him? She had less idea about the technicalities than Don did. 'Don't fret. Luke took her and she's in good hands by now.' She crossed her fingers behind her back. 'Off you go. Tim will be fine.'

Don nodded absentmindedly. As an afterthought, he called 'Bye, Tim!' over his shoulder, and hurried out.

Tim ran onto the veranda and his eyes filled with tears as he watched the car disappear. Amy picked him up. 'When Daddy comes back, you'll have a brother or sister. I've got a brother and I promise you it will be fun.'

He didn't answer and Amy put him down gently. He was silent. Amy found a box of building blocks next to the settee and began to build a tower. After a few minutes, Tim joined in. She felt rather sorry for him; she was almost a stranger and the people he trusted most in the world were all in the hospital. They built a wonky fort and then he said he was hungry. She reasoned she couldn't go wrong with cocoa and cornflakes. The phone rang and she was relieved to hear Luke's voice.

'Just checking. Unless Tim needs me, I may as well wait here with Don. Apparently Judy's doing well.'

'We're okay.' Amy looked at Tim; a little reassurance would help. 'Tim, it's Uncle Luke. Come and talk to him.' She handed Tim the receiver.

Tim was animated. 'Me and Amy are making cornflakes, and then we're going to read Pooh Bear . . . Umm! I will. Promise. Bye!' He handed Amy the phone.

'Hello, Amy. He sounds fine.'

'He's a really good boy, and we're pals.' Tim beamed at her. 'Luke, I do have a problem.'

'Fire away.'

'I want to tell Ruth what's happened. She'll worry if I don't come home soon. I've forgotten their number and can't find a directory.'

'Leave it to me. It will give me something to do.' There was a pause. 'Thanks for helping. Good of you.' There was a click and the line was silent.

5

By the time Tim was in his pyjamas, he was already rubbing his eyes. He intended to wait up for Don's return, but finally gave in to tiredness. Sitting on the edge of his bed, her arm supporting him, Amy had been reading. His eyelashes were fanned across his cheeks and he was now asleep. His body felt heavy and warm. She lowered him onto the pillow, tucked him in, and left the night-light on.

Secretly she was pleased she'd managed to cope, because it was the first time she was completely responsible for a toddler, and there was no one else around to ask what she should do. Now that she could relax, she suddenly found that the silence and the pitch darkness outside the window made her nervous. She switched on the television. The first channel was showing a thriller about a serial killer. That did nothing to calm her nerves. She searched hastily for something less frightening.

Time passed and she heard cars approaching long before they reached the cabin. There was buoyant laughter and Don bounded up the steps. She sighed inwardly and guessed that all was well. She threw the door open and looked at his beaming face. 'And?'

'A girl. Judy is fine, the baby is fine, and the world is just wonderful.' He put his arm round her shoulders.

Amy kissed his cheek. 'Oh, that's fantastic. Congratulations!'

He was grinning like a Cheshire cat. 'Judy's tired, but ecstatic. We hoped for a girl. She's beautiful. She looks like Judy.'

Luke was close behind. He shut the door and said, 'She doesn't resemble anyone. At the moment she's red, she's wrinkled, and she was crying blue murder when I saw her.'

'Rubbish!' said Don. 'You didn't look properly. Believe me, she's going to take this town by storm when she grows up.'

Luke smiled at him and Amy was breathless for a moment as she considered the difference it made to his expression. It made something inside her quiver. Luke was a stranger. There was no reason for her to feel excitement just because he was around. It was probably just the general excitement of the moment. She managed to sound natural when she asked Don, 'So everything went smoothly?'

'Without a hitch. The midwife said it was a textbook delivery.' He looked around. 'I suppose Timmy's in bed?'

'Yes. Do you want to wake him to tell him the news?'

He shook his head. 'Let him sleep. If we get him up now, he'll get so excited we won't get any sleep ourselves. It is celebration time though; follow me!'

Amy did. On the way, he uttered, 'They suggested that Judy stay a day or two just to be sure, and I made her agree. The baby is a little early, and it will do both of them good.' He found a bottle of sparkling wine in the fridge and the three of them settled around the table with their glasses.

Amy murmured, 'I think that's a very sensible suggestion.'

'I think so too, but I'll need someone to take care of Tim. I can take a few hours off tomorrow morning to organise something but we have an emergency order that has to go out, and we have a couple of men sick and off work. Everyone is needed desperately at the moment.' He turned to Luke. 'Judy mentioned you're due to go to Vancouver tomorrow.'

'Yeah! I have a meeting arranged with one of our suppliers and I've been trying to nail him for a couple of weeks. I don't want to call it off, but I'll put it off if necessary. We have to set priorities.' He paused. 'Hey, what about Mrs Mills? She'll help. In fact, I'm sure there are lots of people who'll be willing to help. You only need to ask.'

Spontaneously Amy chipped in, 'How about me? I'll help, if Tim doesn't mind.'

'Honestly?' Don looked hopeful.

'That would be fantastic. My parents planned to be here but no one reckoned with this week. I'll phone them first thing tomorrow; it's too late now. If I phoned them in the middle of the night, they'd get a shock.'

Luke looked up at the kitchen clock. 'It's almost morning anyway. It won't make much difference anymore, will it?'

Don asked, 'Can you take all day tomorrow — er, today? I'll make sure I can be home on the weekend. Perhaps you can take over on Monday too?'

She smiled and nodded. 'Glad to help. I like Tim. It's no problem.'

Don said, 'I can tell that Tim likes you and I'll be very grateful. I can go to work tomorrow as usual and pop in to see Judy when I get home.'

'I think I'll manage fine. He's a lovely little boy.'

'Even if I say so myself, Tim is generally good. Normally I'd automatically get time off. I already warned my boss, but this job came in unexpectedly. If we manage this one, we'll be set up to handle lots of future ones. We had a meeting yesterday when we asked all of the workers not to take time off unless it's an unavoidable emergency. As floor manager I have to set an example.'

'It's no problem. I've time on my hands; I'd like to help.'

Luke looked thoughtful. 'If Tim can see Judy, it might make things easier. I'll take you there to see her before I leave for Vancouver.'

Grey eyes locked with hazel ones, and Amy swallowed. 'Do you have time?'

'Can you be ready by eight-thirty?'

Don added, 'Tim is awake and busy from six onwards.'

Amy blinked and felt light-headed. Despite her intentions not to let Luke impress her too much, he did. 'We'll be ready and waiting.'

Don said, 'It's too late for you to go home now. Stay the night! I painted the nursery two weeks ago and we left it to dry out properly so the guest room is full of the nursery paraphernalia. I intended to put everything back in place on the weekend. The sitting-room couch is very comfortable though, so visitors tell me.' He looked around and smiled widely, then started singing 'Oh What a Beautiful Morning' off key. Amy and Luke smiled at each other across the table. Don lifted his glass. 'Here's to my clever wife and my gorgeous daughter. Here's to Judy and Claire.'

Luke and Amy echoed as one. 'Judy and Claire!'

Don started to reminisce about Tim's arrival. Luke relaxed and Amy had time to study him more closely. He wasn't good-looking in the classical sense — his face was too square and his mouth was too generous, but he was very attractive. She had no plans to get involved with him, of course; she was just visiting Pineville. But she could understand why any woman would be attracted. Amy jumped when she noticed Luke was talking to her.

'Don got totally smashed the day

Tim was born. It's a miracle he didn't get alcohol poisoning.'

Don chuckled. 'Just wait until your time comes round.'

Luke lifted the half-empty bottle in Amy's direction to top up her glass, but she shook her head and yawned.

A smile hovered on Luke's mouth. He looked at his watch, and Amy was thankful when he said, 'Hey, Don, look at the time. I'm off.'

Don was still floating on cloud nine, but he said, 'Okay! Okay! I've decided to phone my parents, after all. Even if I have to get them out of bed. They'd kill me if they figured out I didn't call them immediately. I'll get Amy some blankets.'

When Don disappeared, Luke turned to her and said, 'He's much more sensible this time. Perhaps the euphoria lessens with each baby. Next time he'll probably celebrate with a cup of coffee.'

Her eyes brightened with laughter. 'Next time? Don't dare say anything like that to Judy. She needs to come to terms with this one first.'

His eyes were bright with laughter. 'Yes, perhaps you're right there. Good night.'

'Good night.' She listened to his feet on the gravel, and the sound of his car fading away.

6

Don came back with blankets and a pillow. 'My parents are over the moon.'

'Understandably,' Amy said. 'They won't mind being woken up to hear news like that, I'm sure.' She made up her bed.

'I don't think I'll be able to sleep tonight, but I'll try.' He put out the main lights in the living room and disappeared down the corridor, whistling.

Amy settled down and stared out of the window at the silver disc of the moon shining through the window. It had been a memorable day.

* * *

'Amy, Amy, I've got a baby sister.'

Amy squinted. Tim was level with her face. His eyes were bright and shining and he was hopping with excitement. She gave up trying to cling to the last threads of sleep, yawned and stretched before she ruffled his hair. 'Yes, isn't it great? Isn't it exciting?'

'Daddy says you're looking after me until he comes from work, because Mommy is in hospital with the baby.'

Amy reflected that small children left you no time to slip gradually into the day. She reached for her jeans and pulled them on. 'I'd love to do that, if you let me. We can have fun together. Uncle Luke said he wants to take you to see your mommy this morning at the hospital, before he leaves on business.'

Tim nodded and continued to beam. He circled the sofa, singing louder and louder: 'I've got a sister, a sister, a s . . . is . . . ter!'

Don came down the corridor, his hair still wet from the shower. 'Sorry! I tried to shut him up, but the terror won't keep still and won't keep quiet either.'

She laughed. 'Don't bother. How do

you feel this morning?'

'I still can't believe it. Just wonderful!'

She folded the blankets. 'That's logical. I'll go to the bathroom, then I'll get you some breakfast.'

'Judy was a working mother, so I'm a dab hand in the kitchen. Is coffee okay? I'll grab Tim now and tie him to a chair.'

She chuckled at the shrieks as Don chased Tim around the living room. A short time later she joined them. They were munching slices of toast spread with butter and strawberry jam. She poured herself a cup of coffee.

'How did you organise everything when Judy was teaching?'

'Tim went to kindergarten every day, so she dropped him off on her way to school. Unfortunately the kindergarten is closed for ten days just now, because of burst water pipes. They now only have one useable room and they've confined care to those children who have no one else to look after them. I suppose I could have taken Tim there for a day or two, but it's much nicer for him here with you. When Tim wasn't old enough to go to kindergarten, we had a day-mother for him. By the way, I've just warned Tim he has to be a good boy. I hope that he listens.'

Amy looked at Tim and said, 'I have a feeling he'll make me the second-best informed person on military uniforms in the whole of Pineville, if not the whole world.'

Don chuckled. 'You could be right there. I'm calling at the hospital for a brief visit before I leave for work. I'll tell Judy what we've arranged. Luckily there are no limitations on visiting hours.' He looked at his watch. 'I must be off. Oh, here are Judy's keys. The gold-coloured one is for the front door.' He ruffled Tim's hair. 'Remember to be good. See you this afternoon.'

Tim nodded quite happily. The prospect of being left with Amy didn't seem to bother him. Amy sighed with relief as she cleared the breakfast things and tidied Tim's room. Tim dashed out onto the veranda as soon as he heard a car approaching. She went to join him with the keys in her hand. Luke was squatted beside his car, talking to Tim. Tim's affection for his uncle spoke volumes for Luke's status as a man.

Luke stood up and smiled. 'I've heard all the latest news already. Even what you ate for breakfast.'

Amy felt more awkward with him this morning. He belted Tim into the narrow back seat. She was very conscious of her crumpled appearance and tried to straighten the creases in her blouse. In comparison, Luke looked top-class in his light grey business suit.

'I wonder how Judy's feeling this morning.' She slid awkwardly into the passenger seat.

Getting behind the wheel smoothly, he said, 'Let's find out.'

At the hospital, Luke led the way with Tim holding his hand. Amy followed them down a long corridor. They disappeared into one of the rooms and she sat down outside. Seconds later Luke was back again.

'Hey, what's this? Come on in!'

She swallowed. 'I'm not family. I wasn't sure if there might be restrictions.'

'There aren't. Judy wants to see you.'

He held out his hand. Amy took it and was bewildered by the tingling reaction it produced. She was almost relieved when he let go. Judy was sitting on the edge of the bed with Tim in her arms. She smiled at Amy.

Amy was glad to focus on sensible thoughts. 'Hello, Judy. Congratulations!' She kissed her cheek. 'How are you feeling?'

'I'm fine. Meet Claire.' She indicated the cot alongside the bed.

Amy studied the tiny baby wrapped in a fluffy pink blanket. She was so small, so perfect. Amy was fascinated. 'Don's right — she's beautiful.'

Judy picked up the tiny bundle, supporting the baby's head, and handed her to Amy. The tiny rosebud mouth puckered. The sight of the baby's tiny perfect fingers was awe-inspiring.

'She's absolutely gorgeous. Isn't she pretty, Tim?'

Tim looked sceptical, but he nodded.

'You hold her like an expert — doesn't she, Luke?'

'Don't ask me; I'm not qualified to judge.' The baby gripped his little finger and held on tight. Amy had a lump in her throat. Luke looked at her and then at his watch.

She turned her attention to watching Claire again in fascination — a baby who was less than a day old. Without looking at Luke, she said, 'Tim and I can walk back to Ruth's. I want to get some clean clothes. We'll go back to Judy's from there.'

'I'll drop you off at Ruth's, then, before I leave. Ready, Tim? You'll see Mom again later on, when Daddy gets home from work.'

Tim nodded, and jumped down from the bed where he'd been watching things. 'You're coming home soon, Mommy?'

Judy gave him a kiss and a hug. 'Yes,

promise. Be a good boy for Amy. I'll see you later, okay?'

In the car, Amy was silent. Luke responded to Tim's chatting. When they reached Ruth's she said, 'Don't get out, Luke. I'll manage.' She helped Tim scramble out of the back seat. 'Have a safe journey. Thanks for the lift.'

Luke nodded. 'Oh, by the way . . . ' He fumbled in the glove compartment. 'Here are the keys of my pick-up. It's in front of the house. I thought you might need it in an emergency. Feel free to use it as long as you're in charge!'

She gave him a pert look. 'Do you trust me not to drive it straight into a ditch?'

His eyes twinkled. 'I saw you driving Alan's jeep the other day, so you're not a complete novice.' He looked at Tim. 'If you're good, I might bring you something.'

Tim's expression brightened and he nodded. Luke waved and drove off.

Amy watched his car disappear round the corner and then took Tim's hand.

'Come and say hello to Ruth. Do you know Ruth?'

He looked more subdued, and shook his head.

'Ruth makes smashing cake. We'll have a piece before we go home. She has a budgerigar too. His name is Bluey.'

Tim perked up noticeably. The news about the bird was clearly more interesting than any other information.

* * *

Any worries Amy had about not coping were unfounded, because Tim liked her. After lunch they went to get Luke's pick-up. This time Amy registered the size and shape of his cabin properly. The log walls were bronze; they'd probably darken with age. It blended perfectly into the backdrop of forests and mountain slopes in the distance. It was too big for a single man; it was a homestead for a family.

Amy did some practice manoeuvres

before they drove home. Tim thought it was great fun to go round in circles, and then zigzag down the driveway. It was a good idea to have it waiting outside. Amy hoped there wouldn't be any kind of an emergency, but one never knew. Tim wanted to play football and Amy complied. He fell asleep afterwards. Amy was also glad to doze in a chair. Later Tim played with his cars while Amy peeled some potatoes. When Don got home, Tim ran out to meet him.

Don looked at Luke's jeep and nodded when Amy explained why it was standing there. A short time later Amy slipped into her jeans jacket. 'Your meal is almost ready. You only have to boil the potatoes and vegetables. Tim chose a pie from the deep freeze.'

Don's smile was wide and full of sunshine. 'Thanks for everything, especially for standing in at such short notice.'

She brushed his remarks aside. 'Glad to help; Tim has been a really good pal.' Tim's eyes shone. 'Sure you can manage over the weekend?'

Don nodded. 'Quite sure.'

'Then I'll see you Monday morning. What time?'

'Between half-past seven and eight? I'll pick you up.'

'No need, I'll walk. It's not far. Love to Judy.'

'Thanks, Amy.'

She went, feeling very satisfied about work well done.

★ ★ ★

Monday was another play-day and Tim was happy. After lunch they went for a walk and meandered along a field that ended up behind Luke's cabin. She tried to remember what it looked like inside, but only had vague impressions. She'd been busy with other thoughts that day. Don was already home on their return.

'We've finished the contract, so that means I can have a few days off.' Tim beamed. 'And guess what? I just heard that Mommy can come home tomorrow too. Isn't that great, Timmy?'

Amy smiled. 'What time can you fetch her?'

'Lunchtime, roughly.'

'Then I'll come and tidy up before she gets here.'

'Mrs Mills comes on Thursday.'

'Today is Monday. It will be nicer for Judy to come back to a tidy house, won't it?'

He rubbed his chin. 'Judy won't like it. You've helped enough already.'

She brushed his misgivings aside. 'I'll come about eight. Perhaps you can do some shopping while I do the housework? Ask Judy what she needs. Are you hungry?'

He nodded. 'Of course, I'm always hungry.'

Amy nodded towards the stove. 'You only need to cook spaghetti, the sauce is ready. Tim told me you like spaghetti bolognese and he helped me to make it.' Amy put on her jacket. 'See you tomorrow.'

Amy shared coffee with Don next morning, and then he and Tim went off to the supermarket. She vacuumed the living room, cleaned the surfaces in the kitchen and moved on to the bathroom. She was cleaning the floor under the washbasin when Luke's voice floated over her shoulder. 'What on earth are you doing down there?'

7

His voice, with its soft Canadian accent, sent shock waves through her system. She was taken aback by her reaction and glad he couldn't see her face. When she was in control again, she looked up. He was leaning against the doorframe, arms folded across his chest. Car keys dangled from his hand and he looked amused. The effect he had on her, after a fleeting acquaintance, was ridiculous. Falling for a Canadian — any Canadian — on holiday, would be extremely stupid. 'I thought you were still busy in Vancouver?'

'I was until this morning. Why are you cleaning? Judy has a help — Mrs Mills.'

'She comes on Thursday. Judy's due home with the baby at lunchtime, so I offered to tidy things up before she arrives.' She cleared her throat awkwardly.

'Where's Tim?'

'With Don; they've gone shopping. They'll be back soon.' She looked up into his face, her heart pounding and her pulse racing. She brandished the cleaning cloth in his direction. 'Want to help?'

Feigning horror, he stepped back. 'No thanks.' His voice coaxed, 'I was hoping you'd give me a cup of coffee before I find Jill to give her some information about a derelict paint-works.' His eyes sparkled like gunmetal.

Amy wondered why he was in high spirits. Perhaps his business in Vancouver had been very successful, or perhaps it was looking forward to seeing Jill again. 'No chance! Oh, the keys of your pick-up are on the kitchen windowsill. I didn't use it, but it was good to know it was there.'

'Pity about the coffee.' He tilted his head to the side. 'But if you continue to ignore my thirst, I'll leave you to it. I'll call later to see Judy and the baby.'

Amy had to admit that the business suit, crisp shirt and conservative tie didn't reduce his attractions one little bit — broad shoulders and slim hips. He not only looked good; he generated a warm feeling in her solar plexus.

His expression softened and his voice was genuine. 'It was good of you to help.' Sounding more roguish, he continued, 'Perhaps you'd like a vacation job cleaning my cabin, to help with expenses? Choose your own time; usual rate.'

'No thanks.' She resumed her work.

Luke glanced admiringly at her rounded rear end and smiled. He disappeared without further ado. Amy tried to ignore thoughts of him as his car drove away.

★　★　★

When Don and Tim got back, they all had a quick sandwich lunch together. Amy told Don that Luke had called and would be back to see Judy and the new baby later. He was clearly excited and impatient, longing to fetch his wife and daughter home.

Amy smiled knowingly at him and then donned her jacket. She crouched down to say goodbye to Tim. 'I hope that I'll see you again soon, Tim. Give my love to Mom and your new sister.' He nodded.

Don asked, 'What about giving Amy a thank-you kiss, Tim? She's going home.'

After careful consideration, Tim gave her a sloppy kiss and a hug. Amy felt great.

*　*　*

Two days later Judy phoned her. 'Hey, I expected you to call before now. Tim talks about you all the time.'

Amy laughed softly. 'Does he? That's very flattering. I expect you get enough visitors without me.'

'Some . . . but you were our rescuer, and I want to say thank you personally. Please come!'

'Only if it doesn't upset your routine.'

Judy laughed softly. 'At the moment we don't know what that word means.

I'd forgotten what giving feeds every couple of hours, day and night, was like. But it's not a real problem at the moment because Don is home. Come to see us this afternoon.'

★　★　★

Judy welcomed her with a smile and kissed her on the cheek. 'Thanks for looking after Tim, for providing meals for my men, and for cleaning my house.'

Amy brushed the thanks aside. 'I had time on my hands and Tim was so good. It was a pleasure.'

'But you're on vacation when all is said and done.' She called down the corridor. 'Tim! Amy's here.'

Tim came running down the corridor. Amy squatted to listen to his excited chatter about his sister and what he'd done since she'd left.

'Come and take a peek at Claire — she's sleeping. Don will make us some coffee, won't you, Don?'

Don was behind Tim. He smiled. 'Hi, Amy. Coffee will be on the table in five minutes.'

They went to look at Claire sleeping in her crib. She was all in pink, and looked like a perfect china doll. Amy asked Judy, 'And you're coping okay?'

'Yes! Don is spoiling me. He goes back to work the end of next week.' She tilted her head and the corners of her mouth lifted. 'I don't know how we'll react to a crying baby at three in the morning then. Luckily Tim sleeps through it all.'

Amy smiled. 'I imagine you'll probably feel exhausted.'

Judy said, 'She'll settle down. It was the same with Tim.'

Amy eyed Claire in fascination and Tim toddled off to look for Don. Amy eyed him. 'Is Tim okay? No problems?'

'No. We were worried in case he'd be jealous, but he's been fine up to now. We try to give him some extra attention, and it helps that Don is here to keep him busy at the moment. The kindergarten starts again next week and Don will drop him off on his way to work. That'll give me a breather.' They went back to the living room. Don was putting coffee mugs on the table.

He grinned. 'There! Just how you like it, Amy. With milk, no sugar.'

Judy announced, 'We've decided to have a barbecue on Saturday.'

Amy's brows lifted in surprise. 'A barbecue? Surely you have enough on your plates at the moment?'

Judy shook her head. 'So many people have sent cards and presents. We'd like to say thanks before Don goes back to work. I only need to provide plates, cutlery and somewhere to sit. Don is a brilliant shopper and organiser, and Mrs. Mills and Don do the rest. People always offer to bring something to eat along, and although I normally refuse, this time I'll accept. Do come; bring Alan and Ruth.'

'Ruth will want to contribute something, and naturally I'd like to come.'

'Good.'

Amy listened to their account of the first days of Claire's life and felt almost envious. She got up to go and said, 'I'm going to get some bread for Ruth on the way home.'

Judy nodded. 'We need some too. Don will have to pop out for some later.'

Amy eyed Tim. 'Hey! Why don't I take Tim for a walk, and we can shop at the baker's for both of us. It'll give you both a break for a couple of minutes.'

Tim nodded enthusiastically.

Judy smiled. 'If you like. That would be nice.'

When they were on their way, Tim ambled along comfortably at her side. She asked, 'What do you think of Claire, Tim?'

'She's okay. She's not having my Humphrey though. He's mine.'

Amy remembered him chatting to her about his blue bunny and nodded understandingly. 'I don't think you need to worry about that. Humphrey wouldn't leave you, would he? What does Humphrey think about Claire?'

'He said he wished we'd got another rabbit instead of a baby!'

Amy burst into laughter. They were nearing the road and Luke was driving past. He saw her and noticed her giddy laughter. He drew alongside.

'Hi, you two. What's so amusing?'

She wiped away some tears of amusement. 'Tim just explained Humphrey fancied a fellow rabbit and not another baby.'

He looked bemused for a second and then burst into laughter too.

8

When it was time for them to leave for the barbeque on Saturday evening, the sun was painting the tips of the mountains pink and lilac. There was an invigorating freshness in the air that Amy appreciated more and more the longer she was in the town.

Cars were already parked haphazardly everywhere in the approach field and as they drew closer they could see that the house was buzzing with people. Don was on the veranda, and the grill was already smoking. They eventually found Judy with Claire in her arms and surrounded by a crowd of clucking women. Ruth joined with them and Amy just waved to Judy over their heads and went with Alan to find something to drink in the living room. She already recognised some faces and she also spotted Jill's tall figure among the crowd. She was one of a circle of people near Luke. Against all intents, she felt envious that she wasn't near him too. She wasn't going to be around long, but she already felt so comfortable with Luke that she felt a tinge of resentment that she didn't really belong in Pineville. Since the day she'd volunteered to look after Tim, she felt his reservations had vanished, and that gave her a warm feeling inside.

Amy sipped her wine and focused her attention elsewhere. Next time her glance went that way, he saw her, waved his hand and mouthed, 'Hi!' Amy lifted her glass and smiled back at him. Someone else grabbed his arm and he turned away again. She was merely one of many he knew this evening, and they all knew him better than she did. Amy took another sip of wine and concentrated on other thoughts.

Alan introduced her to a fellow worker. He was an enthusiastic fisherman. After admitting that she knew nothing about fishing, Amy soon wondered how she could steer him away from giving her a graphic description of how to gut a fish. Don saved her as he passed on his way back from the kitchen, carrying a plate of raw steaks.

'The first batch is ready.' He turned to Amy's companion. 'Frank, find Helen and come and get some. Come on, Amy, and sample a real steak à la Don.' She followed him outside gratefully.

Blue smoke rose from the large grill and fat splattered and dripped from the steaks and sausages. She picked up a plate from a nearby pile. 'It looks and smells absolutely wonderful.'

Don smiled at her and deposited an oversized steak on her plate. 'There are lots of salads and fresh bread in the living room. Grab yourself a chair at the table while there's still room.'

She did. A few minutes later Alan sat down next to her, and gradually the long table filled up. Luke, Jill and some others grabbed some of the last places. Amy tried to concentrate on the food.

The steak was perfect; it was very tender and extremely tasty. She reflected that she had enough meat on her plate to feed a family. She listened to the general conversation and tried to ignore the fact that Jill was busy talking to Luke about Vancouver. She looked smart in a snazzy close-fitting outfit. It looked exclusive and special. Where most people were in casual jeans and sportswear, Jill immediately stood out because of her looks and her clothes.

Amy tried to concentrate and noticed that some of the men near her were discussing stricter environmental controls, and the progress that various organisations and indigenous Indian tribes had made in the last couple of years. An elderly man drawled, 'I hear they're cutting in Blind Man's Alley. Heard about that, Luke?'

Amy looked at him and saw his dark brows drawn in a straight line over stormy eyes. He nodded. 'They're entitled to log there. They've followed all the legitimate routes. I've checked, but I'm watching them. We should have organised a local protest and collected signatures before the authorities gave permission. We ought to make it more difficult for them next time, and that means finding out what future plans are in the offing. They have to apply for permission and I presume that we can always get an insight if we keep checking. If we send a petition to the right people, at the right time, it might influence decisions about any future logging in this area.'

The man replied, 'You make it sound simple but it'll end up like it always has in the past. A devoted few of us banging our heads against a brick wall.'

Luke shrugged. 'If that's the only way, then that's the way we'll go. It's no good complaining after decisions are made. We have to shove our boots in the doorway long before it's too late. I think we ought to try to involve the kids at the high school. Their enthusiasm and determination would be a booster. They'd pass on the message to their parents and we might get more support that way.'

Despite all Amy's intentions not to pay him too much attention, Luke's voice set her emotions jingling. She kept her eyes on her plate and cut chunks out of her steak as if her life depended on it. She could tell from the way Luke spoke that it was a subject close to his heart.

Jill said enthusiastically, 'I'll be happy to organise a petition and collect signatures as long as I'm here. Our organisation has lots of experience in that kind of thing.'

Amy mused that although Jill was a newcomer to the community, she was Canadian, an environmentalist, and she was prepared to help. People clearly liked her for that and nodded their approval.

Luke said, 'Thanks, but we already have a functioning group of active environmentalists and this will be a long-term project. We've already organised several past petitions, but we'll be grateful for any additional tips or new suggestions, of course.'

Jill's cheeks were pink and her eyes bright as she looked at him. She nodded enthusiastically and smiled to signal her approval of him and the objectives.

Luke continued, 'We must be grateful for the Boreal Conservation Framework, but that's just the beginning. We need to clean up contaminated industrial sites, support fuel-efficient cars, reduce road salts, keep an eye on the amount of logging, and protect wildlife . . . the list just goes on and on.'

Terry, a friend of Alan's, looked surprised. 'Do we have any contaminated sites locally?'

'Remember that old rubbish dump on the outskirts of Burkedom? It closed donkey's years ago, and it was covered over, but heaven knows what's under the surface. That ought to be checked — I have a feeling the nearby gas station used to dump old oil and used batteries and tyres there. Someone started tipping stuff over the edge into Walker's Gorge years ago. Have you seen what that gully looks like these days? It's packed with old cars, freezers, furniture and god knows what. Then there's that old paint company on the road leading up to the falls. It closed down in the eighties. They cleared out in a hurry. I don't suppose they left it in a decent state. I've only seen it from the fence and God knows what toxic substances are seeping into the ground. Has anyone been there recently? As far as I was able to discover, someone in Vancouver owns the site. Once I've sorted out the details I'll be on to them to clean it up, and I already know that I won't be very popular when I do.'

People laughed. Jill's cheeks were still bright pink and she looked at Luke with an enthralled expression.

Terry said, 'Even if risky sites like that one are cleared, what about the ones that no one knows, or cares about?'

Luke nodded. 'I know. But that's no

reason to ignore the ones we do know about, is it? Think about how the logging companies managed to block out a lot of bad publicity for years, and although we now have some agreements on no-go zones and replanting, we still need to stand on their tails and make sure they stick to the rules. The logging industry is important for Canada, but nature is even more important.'

Jill hurried to support him verbally. 'You're right, Luke. They're scared out of their socks about getting bad publicity.'

Amy managed to restrain from commenting; she knew nothing about the Canadian wood industry or environmental protection. Jill was a member of an official organisation, but Amy's journalistic instincts were irritated. Jill dressed like a director's personal assistant; she didn't look like someone who'd march along a highway waving a banner in the face of authority. Perhaps Amy felt bothered because Jill was possibly interested in Luke on a personal level.

She told herself to be careful and stop speculating.

Amy managed to hold her tongue for a while, but when Jill agreed for the umpteenth time with one of Luke's comments, it drove her over the brink of rational action. She forgot her editor's guidelines about always retaining an impartial view and not getting involved until she was thoroughly informed about the topic under discussion. She joined in, and commented on a subject that she knew nothing about. 'Surely there must be some positive aspects to logging.'

There was a hush nearby, and people eyed her guardedly. Luke waited barely a second. His eyes were hidden in the shadows from the lamplight. 'Like what, for instance?'

It was too late to pull back so, with heightened colour, she ploughed on. 'The companies provide employment, don't they? There must be hundreds of remote places and small towns in the vicinity of logging areas where people are glad of employment, even if it does have negative consequences. When it comes down to it, the only thing most people care about is a paycheque at the end of the month.'

Luke's answering laugh sounded hollow. It disconcerted her, but it was too late to back off. The shadows highlighted the hollows of his cheeks and gave his face a stern aspect. 'You're talking rubbish, Amy. Short-term employment doesn't help small communities, and that's all the logging companies ever offer. They use their own logging teams who go from area to area. If local people get any jobs, they're unskilled, temporary, and badly paid.'

Amy tried to save the situation. 'It's better than nothing, isn't it?'

Luke watched her struggling, but his answer wasn't kind. 'That's your opinion, not mine. People need steady jobs. There may be heaps of permanent jobs in forestry management one day when the forests are under proper control, but at the moment there's still too much logging and not enough long-term government planning. Future generations will curse us if we give up the fight now. There'll be no going back if timber companies destroy Canada's forests. A temporary job with logging companies doesn't solve those kinds of problems.'

Amy's cheeks were hot, and she wasn't grateful for Jill's intervention and attempt to cool the intense conversation when it came.

'You can't expect Amy to understand, Luke. Not like we do. She's a foreigner and when she leaves, she'll go back to a different environment. She hasn't grown up here like you and me. We worry about Canada's future. Why should she care?'

Amy snapped back, 'Don't be silly! Deforestation, HO_2 levels, misuse of energy, and pollution of rivers and oceans affect us all directly or indirectly. But nothing is ever black or white. Greed and selfishness have always existed, and they always will. It'll be hard to convince people about strict environmental controls if it means they have to work harder to feed their families.' Amy steadied her nerves and wished she could fade away into the sunset.

There was still annoyance in Luke's face, but it wasn't quite as marked. He viewed her silently.

Amy shifted to the edge of the chair and wished she could get up and leave, but she didn't know how to do so without losing face. She concentrated on her plate again to avoid Luke's glance. She'd simply antagonised him about something that was close to his heart. Amy was glad he was leaning back and she couldn't see his eyes anymore. She fiddled with her food, which now tasted like dry cardboard.

Alan tried to smooth ruffled tempers. 'Just remember that there are also plenty of Canadians who don't give a damn one way or the other. The Canadian forestry industry is an important export factor and it does provide employment, so Amy isn't completely wide of the mark. Logging needs to be controlled, and at least the companies are being forced into re-foresting nowadays. We need to expand things and make more of an effort though, so that the forests are preserved for future generations. I think we all agree on that.'

Amy nodded gratefully, and decided to zip her lips from then on.

Without addressing her directly, Luke said from the shadows, 'Agreed . . . but it's important never to be complacent or minimise the dangers.'

Amy was heartened by Alan's support and she now had her rebellious emotions under control. She decided to show him she could accept defeat gracefully. With her hands clenched under the table, she said, 'I shouldn't have commented on a subject without knowing the facts, but we need to make compromises in life all the time. If we don't, things usually end in anarchy and bloodshed.' Amy looked down again and busied herself with her food. To her relief the conversation swirled along about other things and without her. She pretended to listen. Somehow, she managed to empty her plate and got up to move away.

Her intervention with unfounded remarks had backfired, and she'd antagonised Luke. Her throat felt dry and she ran her hands through her hair. She met Tim. He was wandering about dragging his blue rabbit behind him and looking lost. He looked up and asked her hopefully, 'Uncle Luke gave me a new rabbit. Want to see it?' Amy followed him down the corridor and pressed the big pink rabbit with its pink bow to her hot face. She was so glad she'd met Tim and could concentrate on his chatter. She played with him for a while and then went to look for Judy to ask her if she could get Tim ready for bed. It gave her something to do, and kept her out of sight. Judy was only too pleased to let her do so. Tim's eyes closed soon after she began to read another of his favourite stories. She dimmed the light and tiptoed out again.

She went out onto the veranda and stood talking to Don for a while. The grill was still busy. She straddled the railing, and a young man joined her and introduced himself as Frank, one of Don's work colleagues. He was the perfect diversion she needed. She felt some of the tension subsiding.

Someone began to play a guitar in the living room and everyone gathered and began to join in the singing. Amy leaned against the wall, thinking how different this lifestyle was to anything she'd known before. There was no artificial camaraderie or pretended enjoyment. During a break in the music, Amy went to Ruth who was sitting with some neighbours. Amy smiled at everyone and said quietly to Ruth, 'I'm off.'

'Oh! Hang on a bit longer, we can go together.'

She shook her head. 'No, please stay. Enjoy yourself. I've got a headache. A walk in the fresh air will do me good.'

Amy slipped away, went down the hill, and through the silent town. She wished she didn't feel dim-witted, and hadn't acted like a second-class journalist.

9

Next day, Ruth and Alan had a long-standing invitation to visit Alan's sister in a nearby town and to stay overnight. When Alan's sister heard about Amy's visit, she warmly included her in the invitation but Amy opted out. She almost looked forward to having a day on her own.

She was in her room when Ruth called up the stairs to tell her that she had a visitor. Curious, Amy skipped down the narrow staircase and discovered Luke in the open doorway, his figure almost shutting out the light. Her cheeks flamed, and she momentarily hesitated before she walked towards him.

There was a frog in her throat. 'Hello! You want to see me?'

Coming straight to the point, he asked, 'Doing anything important?'

The unexpected sight of him confused her. She shook her head.

'I'd like to show you something.'

She was puzzled. 'Now? This morning?' He nodded. 'All right. I'll get my jacket.' She was glad to have a moment's respite to order her thoughts. 'Ruth and Alan are in the kitchen, go through.'

Her stomach was clenched tight. She hurried upstairs, renewed her lipstick and grabbed an anorak. Ruth was cutting and packing some sandwiches.

'Luke said he's taking you on a tour, so you might get hungry. Take something to drink from the fridge.'

Amy nodded. She took the first carton she found, and picked up the plastic container with the sandwiches. She shoved them into her small backpack. 'Thanks, Ruth. Enjoy yourselves.'

Ruth smiled. 'We will. Got a key?' Amy nodded. 'I've left the telephone number on the hallstand.'

Amy followed Luke after he'd said

his goodbyes. By the time she was in his jeep and had fastened her safety belt, they were already on the move. They reached the edge of town and Amy broke the silence and ploughed on with what had bothered her since yesterday. 'I shouldn't have joined in the conversation about logging yesterday. It was stupid of me. I don't know anything about the subject or much about this area either.' She stared determinedly ahead.

'I know that, everyone else did too, and I realise Alan was right. No one expects you to get heated up about Canadian issues. You didn't talk complete rubbish. I wanted to tell you so last night, but you'd already disappeared.' He paused and smiled. 'The Thornton family can't afford to annoy you; you're Tim's favourite person.'

She was caught off guard but uttered, 'I wish I hadn't joined in. I should have been content to listen. I was annoyed with myself later, and I hope I didn't annoy Jill too much. I didn't intend to hassle her, or anyone else.'

'Why Jill in particular? You didn't annoy anyone. It's part of Jill's job to talk about ecosystems and the dangers, every day. She has to state the facts but accept someone else's arguments, and not lose sight of her goal.'

'Yes, but I wondered if she might take it personally. Because you and she are . . . .' Her voice petered out.

His brows lifted and he eyed her speculatively. 'That we are what?'

She stared determinedly ahead and coloured. 'You know . . . more than just friends.'

Luke looked surprised. 'Why do you think we are?'

She squirmed but managed to meet his glance. 'Oh, nothing specific. Just female deduction.'

'So it seems.' Luke laughed softly.

It didn't sound like they were, but she didn't want to nail him, so she asked no more. Amy didn't understand why, but she felt relieved. She closed her eyes and soaked up the sun as they zipped along in companionable silence. The forest was like a never-ending green curtain bordering the road and there was a pungent smell of fir trees as they sped past. Luke asked about her job and pointed out an occasional path in the greenery leading to the homestead of someone he knew.

Amy asked, 'Where are we going?'

'I wanted to show you what we were talking about yesterday. Perhaps it will help you understand better why people are so worried.'

She was just glad he wasn't angry with her. Her mood improved noticeably. They followed the winding highway running alongside a lake and then along the edge of the never-ending forest again. Luke turned off the road down a track. Bouncing along its uneven surface, they passed a cavalcade of long trucks loaded with stripped logs. Luke drove carefully and let empty trucks overtake them. Suddenly he steered his four-wheel drive along a barely visible trail through the rough undergrowth until they faced the opposite side of the valley. He offered her a helping hand to get out and she was glad to feel the warmth and the friendship.

'Come and see what one company's done in four weeks.'

He released her and she followed him. Where they stood and all around them, the forest was still lush and green. Directly opposite it was green to the left and the right too, but in the middle along a vast stretch of land there was just empty ground littered with tree stumps and men working with noisy chainsaws busy among the remaining trees. Another group were extracting the fallen trees to strip and transport to the loading points.

Amy hated the moon-like appearance of the cleared landscape and managed to ask what some other men bending over the ground were doing.

'Planting new saplings. Nowadays they have to. They wouldn't do it unless there were laws to force them to reforest. It's all well and good, but the problem is that my generation won't live long enough to see those saplings grow as tall as the trees they're cutting today. I never wanted to get involved in politics, but sometimes I think it's the only way ordinary people will have a say in things.' His expression was stony.

They watched the retrieval trucks arriving and leaving for a few minutes. The scene and the sound of chainsaws began to grate on Amy's nerves. She viewed the ravaged ground in shades of brown and grey, and wondered if it was necessary. Silently, Luke turned and walked back to the car. She was glad to leave. She joined him and got in. He had his hands on the steering wheel and was staring ahead in silence.

She fumbled with the safety belt. 'It's awful. Especially when you see the comparison of before and after. I'm glad you showed me. I understand better why you and the others feel so strongly.'

He looked across. 'All forests need to be managed and utilised. If they're very lucky they're sometimes left to go wild, but we could save millions of trees if we used less paper. Four million trees are cut down here every year just for making paper. If we used more recycled paper and gave forestry a more sensible priority, then we could reduce the logging. Read much about global warming?'

'Not very much. I know it's about the increasing temperatures, and that it's dangerous.'

He nodded. 'Earth provides its own protective shell around itself, a kind of natural greenhouse. The sun's infrared radiation is trapped there and gases reflect the resulting heat back to earth. More CO_2 means more reflected heat. Plants and animals can't adapt to temperature changes quickly, so they become endangered, or extinct. Trees have a vital function because they convert the CO_2 into oxygen. The more trees, the less carbon dioxide. At present vehicles, planes, factories, and power plants are also producing too much CO_2, so it's vital that we have as many trees as possible to filter the excess. Unfortunately, half the Earth's forests have already disappeared and the amount of carbon dioxide is rising constantly. That's why controlling deforestation plays a major role in fighting global warming.'

Amy decided she ought to be better informed. She'd always been too busy to delve into the pros and cons of environmental issues.

He kept his eyes on the road but added, 'I'm not just concerned about deforestation. We have some examples of bad pollution locally. I hope we can get something done about them soon. I'll show you one of them; it's on our way. It's an abandoned paint firm. Production finished there in the early eighties but they made no effort to clean up before they left. Interested?'

She nodded. 'Of course.'

'It's not far from here.'

She was glad not to have timber trucks in front of them anymore. The memory of the exposed landscape and the never-ending train of log trucks with trees that had stood strong and tall a few hours ago still cluttered her brain. Luke left the road a few minutes later and drove down a barely discernible and overgrown track until they reached a deserted property surrounded by a high wire fence. The fencing was already bent and rusty in places but the entrance gates were securely chained and locked. Glancing at the lock, Amy was surprised to note it looked fairly clean and new.

When they got out Luke said, 'Come over here and take a closer look at the place. There's a gap in the bushes where you can get a good general idea of the layout, and what needs attention.'

She went to stand next to him at the fence. She should be used to him by now but she was acutely conscious of him and his concentrated intensity. Amy jogged her brain into focusing on the task in hand and told herself to remain professional. Her interest should have nothing to do with the fact that this big, lean, tough and determined man was a definite turn-on and she wanted to be with him because he was who he was. Ever since this morning, and every time his eyes met hers, she was beginning to notice a heightened sensation in her insides. She knew very well that she couldn't afford to get caught up in a pointless affair. Falling for him would lead nowhere.

She stared at the site with her nose pressed up against the wiring. Deserted workshops and other run-down buildings that might have been offices, storage rooms or other workplaces were bunched together a couple of hundred yards away from them. They were abandoned and some showed signs that the roofs were damaged and on the brink of collapsing. Long, stringy bunches of grass and rough-looking bushes had gained supremacy over the surrounding terrain. The whole area of the previously tarmacked yard was cracked and split, and was now overgrown with greedy nettles and chickweed.

The tantalising smell of Luke's after-shave reached Amy as he leaned forward and pointed. 'See over there? To the left, the building with the double doors? On the side there's a pile of old barrels, dumped haphazardly and just left to rust and disintegrate. Most of them are already rusted right through. I wouldn't like to imagine what they contained. Note the odd colour of the surrounding earth? I bet that indicates a leakage of something toxic. There's no way of me going in there to check what's happened at the moment. I've got to be careful. The former owners closed it down in the eighties but they still own the place. I already tried to exert pressure on them a couple of years ago, and they got extremely infuriated, to put it mildly. Whoever owns it now would love to prove I entered unlawfully, and drag me to court as a quirky hoodlum who's just causing unnecessary trouble.

'If you look at that building straight ahead, there's a camera just under the roof above the door. They installed that just after I started making enquiries. I've thought seriously about throwing caution to the wind one night, but I don't know how sensitive that camera is, or if the place is wired with a warning system. If I ended up in jail, it would endanger the companies in Pineville and people would be out of work again. I don't know if the camera is even active. Perhaps they just installed a mock version, to keep out intruders. I'll have to find another way to get some proof of what's going on. I wouldn't be surprised if they sent someone to keep an eye on the site, although I've never seen anyone here. I'd love to know what's hidden or left to disintegrate inside and outside the buildings.'

'You're convinced there's a lot more harmful waste than we can see from here?'

'It was a paint factory. In those days,

paints contained a lot of toxic things like lead, cadmium, mercury, arsenic, zinc, nickel, and so on. I'm sure they didn't bother much about what they left behind. Strict rules about ground contamination were nonexistent in those days. And this place is far from any nosy authorities. Perhaps there was bribery involved.'

Amy nodded. 'Do you really think you'll be able to force them to clear it all up?'

'Once I find out who actually owns it. Since it closed down there's been a tangle of original owner, re-sales, subsidiary companies, lessees, and all the rest, but I'll get to the bottom of it one day. They'll fight every inch of the way if I try to nail them, because it'll cost them a bomb to have the place cleaned up. The publicity would be bad for them too. It still belongs to someone, otherwise they wouldn't bother about fencing and locks. I expect they're trying to get rid of it, but no one wants it, for obvious reasons.'

Amy grabbed the rusty wiring and rattled it. She studied the location. 'It's fenced all the way round?'

'Yes, it extends quite a way back. There are piles of barrels, machinery and various stuff dumped all over the place.'

'It sounds like it'll be difficult for you to prove anything if you can't get inside to take photos and get samples. They'd need to be analyzed by an official laboratory.'

He ran his hand down his face. 'I'm hoping that we will be able to do that before they do a superficial clean-up. If they manage to clear away the surface proof, by the time any official inspectors get involved no one will know where to dig. It would be easy to do a superficial surface clean-up and transport any old drums somewhere else.'

'Has Jill been here?'

'I've told her about it. She's busy checking some places on the other side of Burkedom at the moment. She has a list of possible problem areas locally.

She said the paintworks is on her list and she will get round to it eventually. She wants to stick to her schedule, and I can understand that. If every local activist turned up and asked for his particular challenge to be handled straight away, she'd zigzag around like a madwoman.' His forehead wrinkled. He turned towards her and his expression relaxed. 'That's enough bellyaching from me for one day.'

She looked up at him. 'No, I don't mind, honestly. Just because I'm on holiday doesn't mean I shut away from reality.' She gestured towards the deserted site. 'I can understand why you feel angry and why you want to put blame where the blame belongs. If you think they're getting edgy, you ought to be careful. Who knows what they're capable of doing, if you get in their way.'

He threw his arm casually round her shoulders and turned her towards the pick-up. 'You've seen what's bad around here — now I'll show you something completely different. The opposite of what you've seen so far. Do you still have some spare time?'

She masked her pleasure with deceptive calm. 'My time's my own today.'

'Then let's go.'

10

They returned to Luke's jeep, and after a while he turned off the highway again and followed a bumpy track and the signs of faint tyre marks until they petered out completely in an open space. He cut the engine. 'We have to walk from here, but it's worth the effort, promise!'

Amy was curious. Slinging her backpack over her shoulder, she trailed after him and gradually became fully aware of the peaceful surroundings and the atmosphere. Sunbeams danced like specks of gold down through the tall fir trees, and harmless insects swirled around her feet with every step she took. Luke was fitter and his long strides soon left her struggling. He noticed and slowed his pace. Tongue in cheek, he said, 'You're not used to much walking, are you?'

Trying to regain her breath, Amy said resolutely, 'No. We aren't all children of the wilderness. I live in a middle-size town. Where I come from there aren't many chances of long hikes after work and I never fancied jogging my way around pavements every day. If you just downgraded your tempo a bit, I could keep up.' He chuckled and strode on. She was still trying to catch her breath.

He called over his shoulder, 'Remember to watch out for bears. Make noise as you go along. If they're far off they're no problem; up close they can be very unpredictable and dangerous.'

Amy looked around nervously and hurried on. She decided she needed to join keep-fit classes when she got home.

They'd been walking for a while when the ground began to climb slightly. She found the going punishing on her legs and contemplated burying her pride and asking Luke to slow down. Providence intervened. He came to a halt anyway, and looked back. 'You'll be delighted to hear that we're almost there. It's downhill from here on.'

With her hands on her thighs, and breathing heavily, she asked, 'Where are we going?'

'A cabin my father built about thirty years ago. It's one of my favourite places around here and I thought you might like to see it.'

Amy drew closer and saw the roof of the cabin below them, among the trees, but it was the view beyond that that robbed her of the rest of her breath. Like something out of a tourist brochure, a fantastic turquoise-coloured lake was surrounded by snow-capped mountains and edged by lush forests flowing down to the brink of the water. The lake was a gigantic mirror, reflecting the adjacent scenery in its surface. The colours were incredible. She was lost for words as she surveyed it all.

Luke watched her and waited for her reaction. Finally she managed to utter. 'It's unbelievable; absolutely fantastic. The colours are out of this world.'

He looked at it for a moment and nodded. 'I agree, and it looks just as fantastic in the fall, or in winter. Different colours, but the same effect.' He looked pleased. 'Let's go to the cabin. We can have a coffee and enjoy the view from there.'

The lake was lost to sight between the dense trees for a while as they progressed. Someone, presumably Luke's father, had made a clearing for a simple log cabin near to the shoreline.

Luke bounded up the shallow steps and reached for the key on a crossbeam above the door. Amy followed him inside. The room was large and had a big stone fireplace. The furniture looked handmade. The honey-coloured wood was smooth and all the room's other fittings were simple and practical. There were some bunk beds along one wall, and on the opposite side were a sink and some storage cabinets. A second room led from the first and when she looked inside, she found a large rag-rug, a small storage chest and a couple more bunks built alongside the walls.

Luke grabbed the rug and threw it over the rail outside. He explained, 'It gets whiffy when no one has been here for a while. The sun dries it out fast.' He then squatted to open the gas bottle's valve in the cupboard under the sink and picked up the kettle to fetch water from the lake.

In his absence, Amy had time to examine the room. There were a couple of cushioned chairs in front of the fireplace, dog-eared books arranged haphazardly on shelves, a small dresser holding tidily arranged crockery and glasses, and some used magazines and newspapers piled in a corner next to some logs.

When Luke returned Amy indicated towards the stove. 'It's a long way from the road to carry gas bottles, isn't it? I know how heavy they are; my parents have a caravan.'

He lit the hob under the kettle. 'A helicopter brings in supplies for us from time to time. There's no place for it to land so they lower the items in a net, we reload any empties, and they fly them out again. Actually, gas isn't the biggest problem. Drums of diesel are bigger, and harder to load and unload. We need fuel to run the generator and we try to keep plenty in reserve, in case someone gets holed up in the winter. As long as he lived, my father used to handle all that. He had a small sea-plane and brought in supplies that way.'

'Lots of people are pilots in Canada, aren't they? It's not unusual. Can you? Fly, I mean?'

'Yes, I can and I do occasionally, but I don't have my own plane. I promised my mother never to buy one.'

'Why?'

'My father was killed outright when he crashed one day, on a lake on the other side of Sandsville. An empty barrel was floating on the lake, and he didn't see it until it was too late.'

'How awful.'

'My mother never got over it. She

made me promise not to buy a plane, although I sometimes wish I hadn't. She never came here again after he died. They both loved this place and spent most weekends here.' He turned to make the coffee.

She left him and went outside. She threw her jacket over the rail and strolled towards the lake shoreline. Sunshine reflected on the water like specks of undulating silver and gold. The only sound was the gentle swishing of water swirling over the pebbles, or the water shoving bits of wood up onto the shore. The silence was inspirational. Amy thought it would be the perfect place to write a bestseller.

Luke called to her. He was sitting on the steps with a mug of coffee cradled in his large hands, and he had a second one at his side. He appraised her slim figure, the sun picking out the copper in her hair and the multifaceted colour of her hazel eyes as she drew closer.

She climbed the steps and sat down above him. He pushed the mug within reaching distance. Stretching out her slim legs, she threw back her head to catch the sun and then looked at him. 'I've never envied rich people, but I envy you this. It's close to perfection. What about deforestation hereabouts?'

'I'm not rich; this is all inherited. I hope no one ever gets the idea of logging here. Luckily the trees around here aren't valuable, and the only feasible way to transport them would be across land. My father bought up plots here and there whenever he got the chance. The bits he bought look like squares in a patchwork quilt on the map. Building a road for transport purposes would be a nightmare. We're the only ones with a cabin around here. Someone used to have a cabin halfway up the mountain over there, but it's already disintegrating. The people who own it live in Quebec. They have relations in Pineville but they are an elderly couple. They've promised to give me first chance if they decide to sell.'

He pointed to their left. 'The railway sold off various plots along the shoreline to my father for very modest sums. No one was interested in those bits in those days, but it's a different kettle of fish nowadays. Big companies have plenty of money and staying power. I've bought up fishing rights that don't already belong to the local Indians, so anyone would have a hell of a legal battle to change much or drive a supply road anywhere around here. Even one of the narrow strips we own would cause havoc. There's a railway track on the other side of the lake and the railway still owns most of the surrounding land, so that's fairly safe too, especially now when people are more aware of environmental protection.'

'A railway? Where?'

'Alongside the lake shoreline.' He pointed. 'You can't see it from here. Before the highways were built, the railway was the main link between towns and cities in the east. It used to be a busy line. In this day and age, it's mostly freight traffic.'

Amy sipped the coffee. He'd added too much sugar, but it was hot and strong, so she didn't mind. 'And you own the cabin now?'

He nodded. 'My father knew how interested I was in the environment, and he wanted to keep the place as it was. He thought I'd carry on in his footsteps. I don't consider it to be an inheritance in the normal sense of the word. I'm just making sure it and the surrounding area remain protected, if I can.'

'And you come here often?'

'Not as often as I'd like. Other people use it too. Everybody knows we don't object, as long as they stick to the rules. People usually ask if they'd like to stay overnight. They stick a couple of dollars in the jam jar on the windowsill to cover the overheads and that's okay. It's better for people we know to use it now and then, than keep it exclusively ours and end up with moisture damage and a constant smelly atmosphere.'

She looked around and loved it. It was a magnificent place, like something out of a film. She sighed softly. 'What a spot. It's out of this world.'

Disarming her with his smile, he said, 'I thought you'd like it.' He finished his coffee and stood up. Amy took a last sip and got to her feet. Her face was on a level with his. He was a very attractive man; his broad shoulders filled his check shirt to perfection. His muscled body narrowed to slim hips. She wondered what it would be like to be held in his arms.

Biting her lip, she looked away for a moment pretending to focus on the lake again. More balanced, she turned to face him and held out her hand for his mug. 'You made the coffee. I'll do the washing-up.'

Suddenly he leaned forward and kissed her. It was utterly unexpected; the caress of his lips on her mouth set her aflame. It was a heady sensation and she wished its sweet tenderness would go on forever. She breathed lightly between parted lips as they stared at each other silently. Studying the colour of his eyes, her pulse was out of control and her stomach was full of butterflies. She tried to calm her thoughts and reminded herself that a kiss didn't mean much these days. He was just being friendly. She was a tourist who'd be gone again in a couple of weeks. They studied each other for a few seconds then, with heightened colour, Amy looked down at her sensible footwear and tried not to be distracted by romantic notions.

Although he didn't show it, Luke was just as surprised. Having Amy in front of him looking enticing, and so good, had made him act instinctively. He'd never had problems keeping his emotions under control since Kitty dumped him, but now it just seemed like a very natural move. He hoped she wouldn't misconstrue it. He dragged his eyes away from her face, plonked his mug into her hand and hoped he sounded halfway normal when he said, 'I definitely won't refuse your offer to handle the domestic burdens.'

Her throat was dry, but she found that she was calm enough to utter something sensible in return. 'In the lake?'

He nodded and was glad they'd silently agreed to move on. He stuck his hand in one pocket and bounded down the step, then looked up at the sky. 'We've plenty of time, but I'd like to check things in the shed and look around before we leave. Take your time. I promise we don't have to hurry back. We have plenty of time, if you're not under pressure.'

She shook her head and watched him walk away. She skipped down the steps and while she scrubbed the mugs, she busied herself with the thought that she was flattered that he considered her attractive enough to kiss. It didn't mean anything, of course, but it was flattering. Back in the cabin, she dried the mugs and put them back where they belonged. Wondering why it was taking so long, she went to look for Luke.

11

A few minutes later, after moving towards the nearby shed, Amy found him. He was sitting on a tree stump. 'Hey! I was beginning to wonder if you'd left without me . . . ' She broke off. His expression was strained. 'Is something wrong?'

His lips were a thin line. 'I tripped over a damned root, and my foot hurts like hell.'

Surprised, but keeping calm, she asked. 'Can you move your toes?'

He tried to make some tentative movements. 'It's hard to tell in these shoes, but I think so. Hell and damnation! What a dim-witted thing to do.' He pulled up a trouser leg and massaged the area above his boot.

'Don't worry. It can't be helped.' She looked at his sturdy walking boots. 'You need to get out of that shoe fast. We need a knife.'

He was taken aback and his eyes widened. 'What?'

Amy shrugged. 'If your foot swells inside your shoe, it'll hurt even more.'

He looked at her and gave her a lopsided smile. 'You're right.'

She looked at his generous mouth smiling at her, and her insides tingled. She didn't want to remember the kiss, but it sprang automatically to mind again. 'I'll see what I can find. I won't be long.' She hurried back to the cabin, searched the drawers and found a small pocket-knife. Back with him again, she knelt down and said, 'Let's hope it's sharp enough. I'll try not to hurt.'

Amy cut through the lace and pulled it free. The reinforced corners, where the tongue met the side sections, were double-stitched with strong thread. She cut through one side and then the other as carefully as she could, and slit across the stitching holding the leather tongue in place. 'Now's the worst part. Somehow you have to pull your foot out.'

He looked at her. 'That's not a pleasant prospect, but . . . '

'If it was me, I'd do it as fast as possible. It'll still hurt, but I think it'll hurt more if you pull it out slowly. Want me to hold on to the shoe while you concentrate on getting it out?'

Luke enjoyed watching her concentrated efforts and the way she clamped the tip of her tongue between her pink lips, but now it was up to him. 'No. I'll probably see stars but there's no easy way out, is there?'

She was glad she didn't need to watch him. She stood up and turned away, clapping the blade of the knife shut with an audible snap. She heard him draw in his breath and then holler. When she looked down, he was throwing the boot over his head. His face had a greyish tinge and she waited wordlessly for a couple of seconds. The colour returned and she said, 'Whenever you're ready, we'll go back to the cabin.'

He nodded and started to rise. She

reached forwards to help him, and nearly fell over when she tried to pull him upright. He was heavier than she expected. With his arm around her shoulder, he hopped alongside. He spotted a strong-looking stick along the way and asked her to fetch it. He used it on the other side for support and it helped take his weight. They reached the steps to the cabin. He plonked down and gave her another lopsided smile that sent her pulses racing. 'You're a lot stronger than you look.'

Amy went promptly to fetch a plastic bowl she'd seen beneath the sink. She was overwhelmed for a moment when she reflected that they were alone in the wilderness, but she also felt safe and comfortable with him.

Passing him on her way to the lake, she explained, 'Cold water will help reduce the swelling.' She paused and turned to him. 'What about me walking back to the car to get help? How far is your car from here — twenty minutes, half an hour?'

His face froze. 'No way! Don't even consider it.' He rubbed his chin. 'You'll wander off course and get lost. You don't know your way around the forest. We'll wait. Alan will worry when it gets dark. He'll check my place, ask Judy, and eventually they'll come looking and find my car.'

She looked apologetic. 'Ruth and Alan are visiting Alan's sister. No one will miss me tonight, apart from the cat. Did you tell Judy where you were going?'

'Amy! What do you think? We don't live in each other's pockets. Do you have a cell phone by any chance?' She shook her head. 'Neither do I. I left it in the glove compartment. Reception is never reliable here anyway.' He paused. 'I guess we're stuck. We'll have to make the best of it.'

Oddly, the prospect didn't bother her. Luke liked the way she didn't fuss or panic, and accepted the situation as it was. As she scooped water into the bowl she admitted to herself that he intrigued her, and that idea was fraught with danger, because she'd be leaving again in a few weeks.

He pulled a wry face as he submerged his foot in the water. Amy noted that he moved his toes freely, so she presumed nothing was broken. 'Hungry?'

He grinned. 'How did you guess? I'm starving.'

Amy returned his smile and caught her breath. What was the matter with her? She was acting like a star-struck teenager. 'I'll see what I can find.'

'We'd better start the generator too, before daylight fades.'

'If you explain how to do it, I'll have a go.'

'It's not difficult. The generator is in the lean-to. You open the green supply valve on the left, and then press the big red rubber button on the right and hold it down for a few seconds. It might not work first time. Sometimes it takes several attempts. If you can't manage, I'll hop around and do it.'

'Let me have a go first.' Amy had never seen a generator before, and it coughed frantically and died a sudden death several times before it began to run with comforting regularity. The sun had gradually weakened and the lake looked like it was on fire. On her way back to Luke, she went to look for his shoe. After a brief search she pounced on it triumphantly. Holding it demonstratively aloft, she felt extraordinarily light-hearted when he began to clap and whistle his approval.

She clasped it to her chest and beamed. 'You can get it re-stitched and it'll be like new.'

He nodded. 'I've had those shoes for years. A new pair wouldn't be as comfortable. Thanks, Amy!'

'You're welcome! I'll get us something to eat.' She went inside, leaving him staring out across the water.

Amy checked the supplies in the cupboard. She found tins of soup, corned beef and baked beans. There was a sealed box of cornflakes, and some coffee, tea and dried milk in airtight containers. She also had Ruth's sandwiches, some biscuits, chocolate and a carton of fresh milk in her rucksack. She went back outside; Luke was deep in thought. The sun was gradually disappearing behind the mountains and the sky was crimson and gold. She looked across the lake over his head. 'If I hadn't seen it for myself, I couldn't have imagined it. It's unbelievable.'

He nodded silently. 'It is, and bears, beavers and raccoons are still plentiful around here. Nature is fairly okay still.'

'Food is almost ready. Need some help?' She'd like the feel of his arm around her again but also knew that the idea was laced with danger.

'I'll manage.' He got up awkwardly, supporting his weight on his healthy foot, and hopped. 'The water has helped; it feels better already. For some reason you're fated to give the Thornton family a helping hand all the time.'

She smiled at him and said, 'Aren't I the lucky one?'

He laughed and Amy noticed a faint dimple on his chin. She had a ridiculous impulse to touch him. She went to renew the water and then followed him inside.

When she put the bowl down by his foot, Luke said, 'This walk was meant to be a pleasant excursion for you.'

Her eyes sparkled. 'It is. I'm enjoying the challenge. Put your foot in the bowl.'

He did so and yelped. 'It's ice cold.'

'Shut up. It'll do you good. Food's almost ready.'

Minutes later, there was only the sound of their spoons and the hush of shared companionship. The soup, followed by corned beef mixed with baked beans, tasted better than Amy expected. Together with the sandwiches, it was a satisfying meal. She didn't know what they'd eat tomorrow if they were still stuck here. There were still some tins of food but not much else.

Luke leaned back in contentment. 'That was great. Any more coffee?' He looked towards the window. The sun had almost disappeared. 'We'd better start a fire; it gets cold here in September when the sun goes down. Sorry, we need some logs!'

She mused that being shut up with Luke Thornton was a crash survival course, but she didn't mind. She even put up with his teasing comments as she lit the fire. They soon had a good blaze going and she fetched a decent supply of logs from a stacked pile against the outer wall. The room was soon cosy and warm. The fire blazed steadily and Luke made himself comfortable in one of the armchairs.

She ran her fingers through her hair. 'How's the foot?'

'Better . . . I think.'

'I was just wondering about tomorrow.'

'Don't. We'll manage. Alan is bound to start to look when they get back.'

'That's not until tomorrow afternoon, at the earliest. They intended to come back and go straight to work, both of them. Your people will miss you, won't they?'

He shrugged. 'Sometimes I have appointments elsewhere or work from home.' He looked thoughtful at Amy unpacking some sleeping bags and spreading them out to pick up the heat from the fire. She sat down and relaxed with the warmth of the fire on her face. The flames flickered and the sparks hissed and spat and she felt drowsy and content.

'Tell me about yourself, about your family,' Luke prompted.

'There's nothing special to tell. We're a completely ordinary British family.' She let the warmth lull her, and she described the village where she was born and how she'd grown up. She didn't think he was really interested but she liked remembering everything.

'You seem strongly linked to your family and your hometown.'

'Yes, I suppose I am.'

'I presumed you'd be adventurous and ready for change. Looking forward to your new job?'

Amy rested her elbow on the arm of the chair. 'I am in some ways, but I'd rather be going back to my old job.'

His eyes were sympathetic. 'Competition is fierce everywhere these days, but your experience will be useful in other areas of publishing, or even in marketing, advertising, or tourism.' Amy was sceptical but nodded. He continued, 'I started out in banking. Later, it helped me in other ways. A change is a chance to spread your wings and fly in another direction. By the way, I read your article about Pineville in the *Gazette*. I liked it — the way you bridged the past to the present, and how you pinpointed the present optimistic atmosphere. You're a good observer.'

Amy coloured. His praise was unexpected and meant a lot.

He stretched and looked at his watch. 'It's time to go outside and then bunk down. I'll sleep in the other room. The bunks are longer and I'll be more comfortable. You'll be warmer here near the fire.'

'Need any help?'

He looked at her; his mouth curved up and he smiled broadly. 'Amy, there are some things I have to do alone, but thanks for the offer.' He got up awkwardly and found a torch. Supporting himself with the stick, he disappeared.

Amy stared into the crimson flames, listened to the wood spluttering in the fireplace and watched sparks flying up the chimney with the rising blue smoke. When Luke came back, she mused that he now knew more about her than she did about him.

She floundered over the rough ground to the toilet and was grateful for the torch. On her return, the light from the cabin windows glowed in the pitch darkness. When she reached the veranda steps she turned to look at the half-moon, shadow-edged with thin silver reflecting on the lake. She was alone with Luke and the darkness. The sky was full of stars; there was a fresh wind blowing across the water. The air was full of the resinous scent of pine trees. Amy was reluctant to break the spell and go inside.

When she did, he'd already disappeared into the other room. Slipping into the sleeping bag, she called out, 'Do you want an aspirin? I have some in my bag; they'll deaden any pain for a while.'

The fire flickered and sent darts of lights through the room.

His voice was gentle and clear. 'No thanks, I'm fine. There are painkillers in the first-aid cabinet if I need them. Good night, Amy.'

'Good night. I hope you sleep well.' Amy stared at the wooden underside of the top bunk and listened for a while before she finally fell asleep.

12

She woke and found that she was alone. The door to Luke's room was open but the fire was burning steadily, so he was up. Weak sunlight spilled through the windows; she stretched and sat up. Stroking the wrinkles out of her jeans, she ran her fingers through her hair. She ambled towards the door in her bare feet and found Luke sitting on the top step looking out over the lake. There was a grey haze on the water and the sun was a misty outline on the horizon. He heard her coming, looked up and smiled lazily. Her heart skipped a beat. There was a shadow of a beard on his face and she wondered if she felt heady because of the smell of pines or because it had something to do with the time she was sharing with him.

His voice was warm and relaxed. He

looked up and his eyes sparkled. 'Hi. Sleep well?'

'Although it sounds daft in these surroundings, I slept like a log. How's the foot?'

'It's a lot better. We'll try to head back to the car after breakfast.'

'Sure you can manage?' Amy decided she didn't mind if they stayed longer.

'There's only one way to find out. I'm hungry. What have we got?'

'Cornflakes with Ruth's milk, a tin of sausages and baked beans if you can face them again, a bar of chocolate, two pieces of cake, and there are some hard biscuits in one of the tins.'

'Sounds like a feast for the gods.'

'I've found soap and a towel so I'm going to wash. What's the time?'

He glanced at his watch. 'Just after six. I hope I'll find a razor, otherwise shaving will have to wait until we get back to civilization.'

Amy dragged her attention from his face and went indoors to collect the towel. He followed. She helped him search, and they found a couple of disposable razors and a tube of shaving soap in one of the drawers. He set about removing the dark stubble from his face in the spotted mirror above the sink and Amy went to wash herself in the lake's cold water.

A little later they sat eating a very unusual first meal of the day, and talking about what they had to do before they left. Amy felt sorry it was ending and she told herself not to be ridiculous. Luke padded the head of a broom with towels and Amy shut off the generator, raked out the fire, put their rubbish into airtight bags to be picked up later, and shut off the gas. By the time they pushed the mattresses back into their plastic bags, the sun was up. Luke locked the door and restored the key to its resting place, and they began the return journey.

With Luke's arm around Amy's shoulders, they stopped at the top of the incline to look back towards the cabin and the lake beyond. It was a magical place; she'd never forget it. 'I wish I'd had my camera.'

'You can always come back.'

Amy thought that wasn't likely.

They made frequent stops on the way. Luke tried not to lean on her too heavily. They both made light of the situation. Luke thought she was a great person to have around in an emergency — no nonsense, no complaints, and no illusions. When they reached the pick-up, he got into the passenger seat and leaned back. 'You'll have to drive.'

She nodded. 'No problem.' She drove confidently and looked at the clock on the dashboard; it was ten o'clock. She drove straight to the hospital.

When he noticed she wasn't heading for his cabin he asked, 'Where are we going?'

She responded matter-of-factly, 'To outpatients.'

He wanted to protest. His mouth was half open before he thought about it, and then he gave in and didn't.

*   *   *

Amy waited while they took Luke off in a wheelchair to be X-rayed. He came back a little later looking more cheerful. 'It's only a bad sprain. There's nothing broken and no torn ligaments.'

'Good!'

His foot was properly bandaged and he now had a crutch. He made his own way to the car. Amy decided to stop at Judy's. Someone else ought to know, and she was the obvious choice. When she turned towards Judy's cabin, she looked across at Luke briefly and saw he was annoyed, but it was too late. Judy came out onto the veranda wiping her hands on a teacloth. Amy cut the engine and got out.

Surprised, she said, 'Hi, you two. What's this about?'

Amy pointed down to Luke's walking stick and his bandaged foot. 'He's twisted his ankle. We've been to the hospital and they've checked it, but I thought you ought to know.' She told

Judy what had happened.

A muscle in Luke's cheek moved and he uttered, 'Stop fussing. Amy should've driven me straight home.'

Judy glared at him. 'Amy was right.'

Amy thought she was about to witness a clash of wills, but the sound of another car cut things short. Jill got out of her car and joined them. With a smile in Luke's direction, her glance paused when she spotted his bandaged foot. 'What have you done? I've just been up to your place. I tried your office, but no one had seen you, so I thought I'd ask Judy.'

Looking at the three women, he sounded exasperated. 'Before anyone says anything else, I'm fine and I'll manage on my own.'

To everyone's consternation, Jill swung herself, clad in designer jeans and a loose silk top, into the empty driving seat, next to him. 'I'll drive you home and come for my car later. If Luke is up to it, I wanted to show him the wording of an example petition we use before I leave.' Without more ado, she reversed and moved off swiftly. Instinctively, Amy grabbed her rucksack off the back seat as they went past. Luke was protesting loudly.

'Well, I'll be damned,' Judy's voice flared. 'He's not her responsibility, he's mine. How are you supposed to get home?'

Amy swallowed her disappointment. She felt the feeling of contentment fading away. She tried to sound unruffled. 'He'll be okay. Checking her petition will give him something to do, and he'll be sitting down.'

Trying to sound at ease but staring angrily at the departing vehicle, Judy said, 'He was always involved with environmental protection, even when he was at university, but he at least had a steady girlfriend in those days. I never understood the attraction because she didn't care one little bit about protecting nature. Her name was Kitty Sullivan. Ever heard of the Sullivans?'

Amy shook her head and waited.

'Ted Sullivan, her father, is one of the richest men in Canada. He's a multi-millionaire plus. He owns banks, industrial works, media concerns and all the rest. Anyway ... Kitty was a pretty little thing, but she wasn't interested in the environment. She played along because she wanted Luke. One day a group of them planned to fix protest banners about dangerous production methods at a chemical works that belonged to her father. Kitty let it slip at home. Ted Sullivan set Luke an ultimatum: either he pulled out of the scene, or he would lose Kitty. Luke answered by setting Kitty an ultimatum. She had to choose between him and her father. Kitty was used to the good life, and chose her father. Ted Sullivan then started a campaign to defame Luke in one of his newspapers. Luke took the paper to court and won. My parents understood why he fought back, but I think they were very worried in case he lost the case.' She shrugged. 'Who knows if they'd have stayed together, but Kitty's attitude floored Luke. Ever since then he's been ultra-careful about girlfriends or serious relationships. Silly, because lightning doesn't strike twice in the same place.'

'He'll find the right person one day, I expect.' She looked at her watch and slung her backpack over her shoulders. 'I need a shower. It's not far to walk.'

Amy could see that Judy was still disgruntled and smiled at her. 'Bye, Judy. Don't take it to heart. Jill didn't think she was being rude. She just acted impulsively and wanted to help. See you.' Judy nodded.

Alone at last, Amy admitted she liked Luke too much for her own good. Apart from the one kiss out at the cabin, there was no reason to think he'd ever give her more than a passing thought in a romantic way. He was a law unto himself. No matter how much she liked him, there was no way she would welcome a meaningless holiday affair. She walked faster, trying to banish any further thoughts about him. He wasn't hers, never would be, and she tried to tell herself she didn't even want him. When she got home she busied herself with ironing.

When Ruth came, Amy told her what had happened. Ruth's eyes were startled. 'Good thing Luke didn't let you walk back to the car on your own. You would have got lost.'

Amy nodded. 'The cabin is in a wonderful position, isn't it?'

'Fantastic. We go there in winter with friends, for ice fishing.'

'What on earth is ice fishing?'

'You cut a hole in the ice, and fish.'

'You catch fish through a hole in the ice? How mad can you be?'

Ruth laughed. 'It sounds crazy, but it's a popular winter pastime.'

* * *

Next morning, after some soul-searching, Amy decided to phone Luke. Her heart was in her mouth. Expecting to hear his voice, she was dumbfounded when she heard, 'Luke Thornton's place, Jill Edwards speaking.'

She swallowed the lump in her throat. 'Oh hello, Jill. This is Amy.'

There was a pause. 'Amy? What can I do for you?'

'I wondered how Luke was feeling today.'

'His foot is much better. Good of you to ask.'

She clearly didn't intend to bring Luke to the phone. What was she doing there? Perhaps they were still discussing environmental issues. Perhaps she'd been there since yesterday. Amy wished the idea didn't bother her so much. 'Will you say hello from me?'

'Yes, of course.' Amy heard a door bang in the background. 'Have to go, I'm afraid . . . Bye!' There was a click and then a brooding silence.

13

'Choir practice. Coming?' Ruth invited.

'No, not tonight.' Amy wanted to be alone.

'All right, but we'll get you a ticket for the dance on Saturday.'

'What dance?'

'It's a charity event. They're collecting towards a new wing at the hospital; have been doing so for two or three years now. Billy Raynor is contributing some of his paintings for the tombola.'

'Who is Billy Raynor?'

'Billy's our local artist.'

'I'll come to the dance to please you — but don't expect me to stay until the end.'

She decided to visit Judy.

★ ★ ★

'I'm not disturbing you?'

'Far from it. Come in!'

'How are things? Is Claire settling into a routine yet?'

'Some nights are good, others not. It'll sort itself out eventually. Don's parents are coming tomorrow. I'm looking forward to seeing them. They're nice people. They run a hardware store in the next valley. They're dying to see Claire; she's the first granddaughter.'

'I bet they're excited. How's Luke? I phoned next morning to ask how he was. Jill said he was okay.'

Judy's eyebrows lifted. 'Jill? She was there again? What time was it?'

'Just after nine.'

'Luke is usually at work then. I wonder why she answered the phone.'

'Better not ask.' Amy paused wanting to change the subject. 'Alan and Ruth have persuaded me to go to some dance or other in the village hall on Saturday.'

Judy nodded. 'We're going too. Don's parents will baby-sit for a couple of hours. I'm looking forward to it.' Tim came scuttling down the corridor to join them. Judy smiled knowingly. 'Tim, show Amy your new tractor.' She turned to Amy. 'I'll make us some coffee.'

★ ★ ★

Amy had only packed one dress: a primrose-coloured floral summer one that complemented her auburn hair and the colour of her eyes. She spent more time than usual on her make-up and enjoyed dressing up for a change. She'd worn jeans or trousers ever since she'd arrived. Alan whistled and held out his arm for her to tuck hers through his when she joined them.

The vestibule displayed Billy Raynor's paintings. They were talented local landscapes in watercolours. Most already had a 'sold' sign on them. The main room was trimmed with psychedelic paper chains and multicoloured balloons. There was a tempting buffet and Ruth added her contribution to the long table. Amy already recognised a lot of the faces. She mused that the town was so small that the same people turned up at events, all the time. She felt at home and comfortable, and lots of people smiled and said hello. CD music was alternated with live square-dance music by a local trio. The fiddler, accordion player and guitarist produced a loud foot-tapping sound that brought most of the people onto the dance floor.

She strolled around the room and eventually met up with Judy and Don. Don was leaning against a convenient post and viewing the goings-on. Amy whispered, 'Don told me he could take the polish off any dance floor. At the moment, he just looks worried. Was he just bragging?'

Judy laughed and said, 'Probably! Once he gets going he's not bad.' She spotted a tall figure making his way through the spectators. 'Oh, Luke. That's good. I wondered if he'd make the effort.'

Amy's colour automatically increased. She noticed he wasn't limping very much anymore.

He nodded to Don and Judy and

eyed her blandly. 'Hi, Amy. Didn't think this was your scene. Like dancing?'

Just the sound of his voice made her insides quiver. The more she saw him, the more complicated things got. 'No, not much. Ruth and Alan dragged me along. I see the foot is a lot better.'

Judy grabbed Don and pulled him onto the dance floor. Alone with Luke, Amy tried to calm her racing pulse. Her throat was dry and her nerves tingled. Without the slightest effort on his part, Luke overwhelmed her again.

'Much better, thanks to you. Sorry, I didn't know you'd phoned until Judy told me this afternoon. Jill answered the phone. She called for some papers I'd sorted out for her. I was probably in the kitchen at the time, and it slipped her mind.' His gaze moved over her appreciatively. 'I don't think I've ever seen you in a dress before. Very impressive!'

Amy's mood improved by leaps and bounds. He went to get them something to drink and returned as the current dance series ended.

Don and Judy grabbed the drinks from him and drank thirstily. 'Just what we needed.'

'Hey, I had to fight for those.' Luke held out his hand to Amy when some slow music began. 'They've pinched our drinks; we'll leave them to it. Dancing is not one of my favourite pastimes, but I can manage this. I'll try not to trample on your feet.'

She was silent until she was accustomed to the feeling of the hard muscles of his body so close to her. They moved in languid circles to the slow music. The top of her head reached his chin. When he looked down, the dimple appeared and a crooked smile. She cleared her throat. 'You manage very well, and haven't stood on my feet once so far.'

He held her snugly and replied, 'Don't trust your luck too long.'

Amy had a giddy sense of pleasure. She forgot about controlling swirling emotions, and enjoyed the warm glow of just being with him. When the music finished, he kept her hand in his. Amy didn't pull it away; it felt right.

On the way back to Don and Judy, some people stopped them to talk to Luke. Amy listened politely, glad that she had a respite to quieten the hammering of her heart. One of the younger men in the group caught Luke's arm and pulled him towards the makeshift bar. He dropped her hand and gave her an apologetic look. She smiled, shrugged, and left him to his fate.

As the evening continued Amy danced with Don, Terry, and Alan. She watched the others for a while, and joined in some entertaining party games. The room was hot, and full of music and noise. Amy went to look at the paintings again. It was welcomingly quiet in the vestibule. She decided to go. She'd had Luke to herself for a few minutes; that was enough.

Ruth nodded understandingly when she told her. Don and Judy were talking to another couple on the other side of the room. Amy caught Judy's eye, laid her head on her hands and pointed to the door. Judy waved. She didn't look for Luke.

She pushed the door open, felt a rush of cold air and shivered. She paused and waited for her sight to adjust to the meagre lighting. Someone was sitting on the surrounding low brick wall, one leg on the ground, the other resting at an angle on the wall. She could tell it was Luke. Her shoes were silent on the flagstone path. He was looking towards the town, so she thought he hadn't noticed her.

'Deserting the festivities?' He looked up; his face was hidden in the shadows. 'The noise is deafening in there, isn't it?'

'Yes; everyone is having a good time though. It was more fun than I expected but I've had enough.'

He stood up and brushed the seat of his pants. 'I'll take you home.'

'There's no need for that. I'll be

perfectly all right on my own.'

'I know that. I'll leave my car here until tomorrow. I've had a couple of beers. I'll just check that it's locked.'

There was no point in protesting, and Amy welcomed his company. She waited. Satisfied, he took her arm. 'Brr! You're a block of ice,' she said.

'My own fault; I didn't think it'd be so cold.'

He re-emerged from the car boot with a sweater. 'Here, put this on; it'll save you from frostbite. September is a lovely time of year, but now towards the end of it, the evenings are getting noticeably colder.'

Amy pulled it over her head. She registered Luke's spicy aftershave. The sweater was like an oversized sack. He studied her in the lamplight.

'It's not very flattering. You look like a tube-shaped sheep, but it'll keep you warm.'

She laughed. 'I hope you mean the body part and not my face as well, although sheep can sometimes be very endearing, can't they?'

'I assure you, you're the best-looking sheep I've ever seen.'

'I feel warmer, and I don't care what I look like.'

They started out. The sky was plastered with stars.

'Has Pineville changed a lot since your childhood?'

'Places change continually, don't they? People change and their attitudes change. This morning there was a break-in at my office; that would never have happened twenty years ago.'

'You mean a burglary? Anything stolen?'

He shrugged. 'What's worth stealing from a small company? It's hard to tell. The computer is fairly safe because of passwords and so forth, but industrial spies look for things that you take for granted.'

Her eyes widened. 'Industrial spies in a place like Pineville? Have you reported it?'

He nodded. 'Merely as a matter of

form. There's no proof that anything was stolen. It could just be kids larking about.'

'But annoying.'

They went in comfortable silence, and then Amy asked him about his parents, about university, and about his plans for winter tourism. They passed the Blue Bear; it was relatively quiet. When they reached Ruth's house, Amy felt the walk had ended too soon. 'I feel guilty about you coming all this way.'

'Why? I wouldn't have come if I didn't want to.'

He said what he meant, and did what he did without apology or explanation. She liked him . . . perhaps too much. She hesitated. 'W . . . would you like something to drink?'

'Why not?' He followed her into the kitchen. Amy removed the sweater and he helped her. His eyes held hers and he reached up and stroked some unruly strands of hair back into shape. His touch confused her and she turned away.

'Coffee? Tea? Something stronger?'

'Coffee will be fine.'

His eyes followed her until they were both sitting. He broke the silence. 'I never thanked you for coping so well at the cabin. I should have bought you flowers or something.'

She shook her head. 'To be honest, I enjoyed it. I was only scared in case I ended up gutting fish, digging for roots and collecting berries to keep us alive.'

A deep chuckle progressed to laughter. She laughed too. 'There wasn't much food left so we would have had to do something. Have you been back since?'

He shook his head. 'I don't have time to go there often. We, or more exactly you, closed everything down properly, so there's no rush. Knowing what happened to us, I think I'll boost the amount of emergency rations we keep there from now on. There are lots of foods that keep a long time these days.'

'And perhaps a signal gun for emergencies?'

'That shouldn't be necessary in this age of cell phones. I just didn't have mine with me. I don't suppose anyone would even see a signal like that, unless they were out in that part of the forest.' He looked at his watch. 'I'd better go. I've a meeting with someone from a construction company early tomorrow morning.'

'On a Sunday?'

He got up and picked the sweater up from the back of the chair. 'Some people are too busy on site during the week, so it has to be Sunday.' He shrugged. 'That's the way it goes sometimes.'

Amy followed him down the hall. He stepped out into the dim porchway, then leaned towards her and her stomach knotted. It was impossible to steady her erratic pulse. She was waiting in silent expectation and a prickle of excitement fretted her skin.

They heard the click of the garden gate and he straightened. He said 'Night' before he turned away abruptly.

Amy heard him talking to Ruth and Alan. She controlled her disappointment about what might have been and went back to the kitchen.

She busied her hands with their mugs and while Ruth was filling the kettle, she asked, 'Want something to drink, Amy?'

'No, thanks. I just had coffee with Luke. It was fun tonight. You seem to have enjoyed yourselves too. I'll turn in.' She turned to go.

Ruth's eyes were clouded. 'Amy . . . you and Luke . . . It's none of my business, but don't get hurt.'

Amy managed to sound cheerful and unconcerned. 'Don't worry, I won't. We're just friends.'

Climbing the stairs, she hoped Ruth believed her. She knew she was sliding down a very slippery slope. If she encouraged him, it would be a holiday affair with no strings attached. Amy knew she didn't want that. She wanted the love of a lifetime. Perhaps it was time to leave Pineville, before she got too entangled with a pair of grey eyes and a tempting smile. Perhaps he had another girlfriend somewhere, or his interest in Jill was more than it seemed on the surface. It was more sensible to avoid him. She'd go to Vancouver for a few days. That would help, and she'd be going home soon. Reassured, she closed the curtains and got ready for bed.

14

Next evening, fate intervened. When they were sharing the evening meal, Alan announced, 'I'm going to Vancouver to pick up some company stuff on Friday. You wanted to go, didn't you, Amy? How about coming with me? You'll save some fare.'

Her face brightened. 'Really? I was thinking about Vancouver last night. It would suit me just fine. There's no problem in taking me along?'

'I have to clear it with the office, but people often come along for the ride.'

Ruth and Alan hadn't been to the city for a while and suggested she book a hotel via the local travel agency.

Next morning she was walking towards the agency along Main Street, when someone tooted their horn. Judy lowered the car window. 'Where are you going?'

'I'm on my way to book a hotel in Vancouver.'

'Oh, lucky you. All those wonderful shops.'

'Where are Tim and Claire?'

'With my parents-in-law. Come shopping with me, and then I'll take you home and give you a city guide and the details of the hotel where we always stay.'

Amy got in. Judy bustled up and down the hypermarket aisles, filling the trolley with family-size items until it was overflowing. Meanwhile, she told Amy about Vancouver.

Back at Judy's cabin, Tim was having a great time with his grandfather on the floor. Amy squatted to ruffle his hair. 'Hello, my friend. Having fun?'

He grinned and giggled. 'Yes, playing submarines.'

Don's father smiled. 'I'm about to be torpedoed again.'

Amy smiled. 'I know the feeling.'

Mrs Harrison remarked, 'You're on vacation?'

'Yes, but I'll be going home soon. I want to see Vancouver before I leave.'

'Life would be wonderful if it was just one long vacation, wouldn't it? We have to open the shop again on Monday. I wish we could stay here with the children.'

'One day Judy will put them on the bus and you'll be able to pick them up on your end.'

Judy came back. 'Here you are — a hotel prospectus, a street map, a travel guide and some bus timetables, although they're probably out of date.'

'What should I see?'

'Stanley Park, Gas Town, China Town, go out to the Anthropological Museum at the university, browse around the shops. Oh, I do envy you.'

'Need anything?'

'Could you bring me some perfume? I can't get it locally.'

'No problem. What's it called?'

Judy scribbled the name down quickly. 'Come and tell me all about it. Coffee?'

'No, I have to go.' She looked down

at the paper. 'I can book this via the internet. I don't need a travel agent anymore. Bye, Mrs Harrison, Mr Harrison. Nice to have met you.'

Mrs Harrison's eyes twinkled. 'Likewise. You'll love Vancouver, everyone does.'

Judy went out onto the veranda with her. 'I hope the weather holds, but pack a sweater. The evenings will be cool.'

* * *

On the way home, Amy bought some groceries for Ruth. She was deep in thought and jumped when Jill called her from the drugstore entrance on the opposite side of the road.

Politely Amy said, 'Hello, Jill. Shopping?'

Jill came across. 'Oh just a couple of items, you know how it is.'

Amy wasn't in the mood for chit-chat. Jill was too polished and they had nothing in common, apart from an interest in Luke. Even this morning, she looked too well-groomed for a provincial town. The shoes and handbag were perfectly matched to the trimmings of her pink tunic dress. Her make-up was flawless, and she had small stud earrings that glistened in the sunlight.

Amy searched around for something sensible to say but Jill was quicker. 'You were at the dance on Saturday?' She looked down at her perfectly manicured nails. 'I was invited but decided not to go. Spending time square-dancing with locals isn't my idea of fun.'

Amy's hackles rose. 'Isn't it? But it was fun.' She couldn't help adding, 'Even Luke seemed to enjoy it.'

Jill tried to sound less belligerent. 'I know. It must be dreary for Luke to live in a small community like this. Everyone expects him to support things and put in appearances all the time.'

'I got the impression that he goes because he wants to. People like him for what he's done for the community, and they all know him; he grew up here.'

Jill adjusted her shoulder bag and

eyed Amy belligerently. 'My, my, we are championing him, aren't we? I'm sure that people bother him all the time. He's just too polite to give them the cold shoulder. Considering that you're a stranger to the town, you're not really in a position to judge what goes on, are you?'

Amy was silent and stared at Jill for an angry minute. The colour was high on her cheeks 'And you are? You don't know him or Pineville any better.'

'Ah, but I do. What he thinks, what he loves — more than most people suspect.' Her voice faded and she stared back with a meaningful expression.

Amy looked away and took a deep breath. This was stupid. Why was she arguing with Jill about Luke? 'Let's agree to differ, but you're definitely mistaken when you think local people are stupid and boring; they're not.' Jill didn't answer.

Someone sounded the horn and they both looked up. Luke's car was passing. He stopped further down the street, in front of the bank.

'Oh, there's Luke.' Jill looked at her watch. 'He's early. Bye, Amy.' Her voice was all sweetness.

Amy didn't answer; she moved on and didn't look back. She didn't see how fast Luke had disappeared into the bank.

Jill flushed, but a glance in Amy's direction reassured her. Amy wasn't looking. She didn't like the way Amy was fitting so effortlessly into the community and making inroads with Luke. She needed to get going, and wheedle her way into Luke's life faster than she expected. She lingered at a revolving stand with postcards outside a nearby shop until she saw Luke coming out.

15

Alan dropped Amy off at a Skytrain station, helped her to get a ticket, and left her. The journey to Waterfront Station in Vancouver was fast. Amy already knew the streets were laid out like a grid, so it was easy to follow the plan and find the hotel. She looked around at the panelled woodwork as she waited for the receptionist to check her booking. The woman handed her a key.

'Breakfast is from six-thirty until ten. The lift is to your left, and your room is on the third floor.'

Amy nodded and picked up her holdall. 'Thank you.'

She unpacked quickly and then walked down to the harbour area with its famous skyline. A nearby tourist office provided her with up-to-date timetables and guides. She drank coffee, ate a muffin and watched people passing. Using the guide, she walked through Gas Town and bought some Canadian souvenirs for the family. She stopped for a meal at a self-service restaurant on the way back to the hotel. Daylight was fading and the city's façade sparkled as the lights of the various districts flickered to life.

Next morning her eyes swept the breakfast room looking for an empty table. She couldn't believe it: Luke was sitting by the window. He patted the chair next to him. Her mind froze and her mouth opened. She closed it fast, and followed his invite.

'Hi, Amy! Yes, it's me.'

'W-what are you doing here?'

'On business. I'm not surprised to see you; Judy told me you were here.' He bundled some papers together and shoved them into his briefcase. 'I've been sorting out my strategy on how I'm going to handle a supplier who hasn't delivered some important equipment, and after I've been there I'm off to meet someone from a company who might include Pineville in their winter catalogue. Have some breakfast.'

Slowly her brain began to function.

A waitress brought Luke a cooked breakfast. As if it was perfectly natural for him to be facing Amy across the breakfast table, he said, 'Have a hot breakfast if you're going to wander round Vancouver all day. There's a lot more on offer than we had out at the cabin.'

The waitress pulled out a pad and a pencil. 'What would you like, miss?'

'Egg and bacon, please.'

Luke picked up his cutlery and said, 'Fruit juice and cereals are over there.'

Amy slung her bag over the back of the chair and went. His eyes followed her. She was slender without being skinny, very attractive, and a nice person to boot. When she came back he asked, 'What do you think of Vancouver so far?'

She cleared her throat. 'I only got here yesterday! What I've seen is great.'

'What's on your agenda for today?'

'I think I'll look around the city centre and go to the Anthropological Museum. I'm very surprised to see you here. Judy didn't mention it when we spoke.' Even though Amy felt calmer, every time his gaze met hers, her heart flipped.

The contents of his plate vanished rapidly. The waitress brought Amy's plate of cooked food and some toast for Luke. He buttered the toast generously and took a bite.

'This is definitely more luxurious than the last time we shared breakfast, isn't it?' Amy nodded. 'I don't expect my business will take long.' He paused. 'Then I'll be your guide if you like. You can wander around the centre for a few hours, and then I'll take you out to the museum.'

Amy thought about Jill and said instinctively, 'As long as I'm not stopping you doing something else that you've planned.'

He looked taken aback and puzzled.

'I'm free as a bird to spend time with whoever I like.'

Her emotions soared. 'In that case, I'd like your company.'

He gave her a lazy smile and glanced at his watch. 'I suggest we meet at the corner of Robson and Howe, and The Bay. Got a street plan?'

'Yes.' She fumbled in her bag and he showed her where. 'What time?'

'I don't suppose the meetings will take very long. Eleven? That gives you a couple of hours to look around the shops. Will it be enough?'

Amy felt quite heady. She pushed all thoughts that it wasn't sensible to spend time alone with him from her mind. 'Fine.'

He picked up his briefcase. 'I ordered a taxi for eight-thirty. I'll see you later?' She nodded.

He wound his way through the maze of tables and raised his hand before he left. She relaxed and finished her meal.

★ ★ ★

A little later, she checked the map again and left the hotel. The sun was shining and she visited the main shopping malls. It was a complete contrast to the quiet and cosy atmosphere of Pineville. She wandered through one exclusive department store after another. Everything imaginable was on offer. She bought Judy's perfume in one of the stores and gradually wandered towards their meeting place. Time passed quickly. She saw Luke before he saw her. He'd changed into chinos, and he had a navy jacket slung over his arm.

When he saw her, he smiled. 'You're punctual. What have you bought?'

'Perfume for Judy, and a couple of postcards.'

'You've been shopping for a couple of hours, and that's all?'

She smiled. 'There are lots of wonderful things, but I can't afford them.'

'I've bought you something.' He handed her a small paper bag.

Amy was taken aback. 'Why? What for?'

Laughing grey eyes met confused hazel ones. 'Do you need a reason? Don't look a gift horse in the mouth.'

Amy extracted a silk scarf. The colours matched her sweater. 'I don't know what to say.'

'Then don't say anything.' He tied it around her neck with a loose knot. It lay in gentle folds and he said, 'It looks good.'

'I'm sure it does.' It was hard to stay coherent when he was so close, but she tried hard. 'Thank you, Luke. I haven't done anything to deserve it.'

He stepped back and eyed her carefully. 'Let's catch the bus. Do you have some small change, by any chance? The drivers expect the right money.'

Amy felt a growing elation. 'Here.' She handed him her purse.

He weighed it in the palm of his hand. 'Good Lord, it weighs a ton.'

She laughed. 'It's easier to change a note than to figure out the various coins. It mounts up.'

They joined the bus queue. When it arrived, Amy claimed an empty seat; Luke paid and joined her. He gave the purse back to her. 'Not made a lot of difference, I'm afraid.'

'How did your meeting go?' His mere physical proximity made her feel woozy.

His mouth turned up in a lazy smile. 'Not bad; nothing definite, but the tourist chap didn't turn us down outright. He wants more information and more time to think about it. We're meeting Monday before he leaves.'

She paused. 'That means you go home and come back again on Monday.'

He shook his head. 'It's not worth it. There's nothing special I need to do at home, so I hope we can enjoy the time here together.'

Amy swallowed the lump in her throat and smiled. 'That sounds good.'

The bus wound its way slowly through the suburbs.

'I expect you know this route by heart?'

He shrugged. 'Yes, but there was plenty going on at the university. I didn't go into town that often.'

'You enjoyed university?'

He nodded. She'd relaxed by the time the bus reached the end of the route, and he pointed out various buildings. 'This is all part of the university.'

The waters of the bay glittered through the buildings, and the mountains soared in the background. 'It's a fantastic setting for a university, isn't it? Where are the students' quarters?'

'Over to the left. The museum is along here.'

When they reached the museum buildings, she insisted he pay from her purse again. It was much lighter afterwards and he spun her around to push the purse back into her backpack. 'This is great — a woman who pays the bill. The last time that happened to me was when Jeanette Carter thought she could tempt me with a banana shake in junior high.'

Tongue in cheek, she said, 'Jeanette must have been bonkers. I hope she got her money's worth.' Amy picked up a leaflet showing the museum's layout.

'Why don't you just wander around on your own? I don't know more about the things than is written on the labels. I'm going to read my newspaper.'

'Okay.'

'Take your time. It's luxury for me to have nothing to do.'

Amy puzzled over many things, but it was extremely interesting. Two hours later, she made her way back to the Great Hall and found Luke with closed eyes and his legs stuck out in a straight line. She edged closer and took a photo, saying, 'You look like a cat basking in the sun.'

He moved and opened one eye, then the other. 'Was it worth it?'

Amy threw herself into a neighbouring chair and began to massage one of her feet. 'Very. But there's so much to see.'

'There's a special exhibition of

Chinese pottery through that archway. I had a look; it's very impressive. Want to take a peek?'

Protesting, she said, 'My feet are killing me.'

'So you've had enough culture for one day?'

She nodded. They went outside and strolled to a bench overlooking the waterfront. Straggly bushes sheltered them from the sea breezes. He ate some chocolate and she chewed on an apple in the afternoon sunshine. When he finished he screwed the paper into a silver ball and tossed it into the bin. 'Give me your camera. I'll take a photo — or does it have a self-timer?'

She nodded. 'It does; that tree trunk will do. I'll set it.' Amy handed him her half-eaten apple, set the timer, and rushed back to the bench. She started to laugh and he threw his arm around her as she flung herself down. A red light flashed. Laughing and looking at him, the camera clicked. His face was close and she grew silent as he kissed her. The touch of his lips was as tantalizing as the first time, that day by the lake.

He broke the silence. 'I'd like a copy of that, please.'

His fingers skimmed her cheek. Amy tried to analyse the fleeting emotion in his face. She bent to steady her thoughts, ruffling through her backpack. 'Want an apple?' Her cheeks were pink when she looked up.

'No.' Amusement was in his eyes. 'That's what brought Adam to his knees.'

She collected the camera, to give herself time to calm down.

When she returned, he said, 'The bus is due in a couple of minutes.'

On the way to town, they talked of routine matters: about Claire, about Pineville, about his plans for the winter ski lift. They talked about everything and nothing. She was content to be with him. Amy didn't want to think about tomorrow, next week, or next year. By the time the bus reached the city, daylight was fading.

'Want to go back to the hotel before we eat?'

'It depends where we go. Do I need to change?'

He shook his head. 'Like Italian food?'

'Love it.'

'There's an Italian restaurant in Gas Town — the best there is.'

He tucked her arm through his and they joined other people ambling towards Gas Town. Amy had an excuse to cling to him. When they reached the small restaurant, she found there were a couple of tables outside. Cool winds from the harbour ruffled the tablecloths and pots of crimson geraniums decorated the small windowsills and waved in the sea breezes. Luke ducked his head and went inside.

A short, stubby, dark-haired man hurried over, reached up and grabbed Luke by the shoulders. His voice was volatile. '*Come stai, Luca?*'

'*Bene, grazie.*'

Machine-gun chatter in Italian followed. Luke pulled Amy forward and draped his arm around her shoulders. 'Carlo, this is Amy.'

Amy smiled at him. 'Pleased to meet you.' She held out her hand.

Carlo took it, lifting it to his lips with Latin charm. His eyes assessed her. 'Any friend of Luke's is a friend of mine.' They were directed to a corner table and Carlo lit a red candle in a Chianti bottle. He brought them a grappa. Carlo chatted to Luke until he had to bustle off and serve another customer.

Luke looked up from the menu. 'Want to choose, or leave it up to me?'

'I'll leave it up to you. You speak Italian?'

'A smattering. I worked here sometimes to earn pocket money. It's a family business, in the third generation. They still speak Italian among themselves.'

Carlo smiled at Amy as he took their order. The flames from the candle wandered across Luke's face. He'd probably been here with lots of other girls before. She fiddled with her serviette.

He seemed lost in thought before he asked, 'When are you going home?'

'I haven't booked yet, but . . . ' Carlo interrupted them with minestrone soup. ' . . . soon I expect. I need to find somewhere to live before I start my new job.'

'So your new workplace isn't in your hometown?'

Amy shook her head. 'My last one wasn't either. This one is even further away, in Bath.'

'Will you miss your family?'

'Yes. Families are a rock in life's storm.'

'So you're not planning to knit socks for your own family for a while?'

Amy would like to have said 'I'd consider doing that for you,' but she didn't. She chuckled. 'Not at the moment.'

'And you won't miss Pineville?'

She avoided his eyes and drew invisible patterns on the tablecloth. 'I'll never forget it. I might even come back one day — who knows.' She looked up and took a deep breath.

Carlo returned with the main course. He stopped to chat whenever he had a moment to spare and insisted that they say hello to the family before they left. The kitchen was dominated by a large central cooking range. Amy listened to the chatter and Carlo's wife handed her a glass of amaretto. Amy sipped it and stored the memory of Luke talking to them. Carlo shook hands with Luke and kissed Amy's cheek. 'Come back soon.'

'Thank you, Carlo. The food was wonderful. If I ever come back, I will come here again, promise.'

They weren't in a hurry even though the breezes were chilly and heralded much colder days to come. When they entered the foyer, Luke said, 'Shall we . . . ?'

The receptionist interrupted. 'Good evening, Mr Thornton. A message for you.'

Luke read the note. 'That man wants more details about Pineville. It's late, but perhaps he's still awake.' He said to the receptionist, 'Get me the number, please.'

Amy said, 'Thanks for a lovely day. It was great. Hope you can sort things out.'

'So do I; this is important for Pineville's future.' He paused. 'I thoroughly enjoyed today.'

'So did I.' Amy kissed his cheek before she went to the lift.

The receptionist called out, 'Mr Thornton.'

16

Luke had almost finished breakfast by the time Amy joined him next morning. His eyes skimmed her dark trousers, the silk sweater and his scarf wrapped loosely round her neck.

'Morning! I thought I'd be early but you beat me to it again.'

He folded his newspaper.

'I'll stick to orange juice and corn-flakes this morning. I'm not hungry after that wonderful Italian food last night.' She noticed his empty glass. 'More juice?'

'No thanks. What were you planning for today?'

'Stanley Park. Judy said it has a zoo and an aquarium.'

'The park's sizeable, but the zoo and the aquarium aren't very big. Still . . . ' He shrugged. ' . . . if you want to see them, we'll go there before the weekend crowds start to pour in.'

'Did you contact that man afterwards, or was he already asleep?'

'No, he was still awake. I sent him the information by taxi.' He glanced out of the window. 'It's good weather again. You're lucky; it rains a lot in Vancouver.'

They strolled to the bus stop. Amy still couldn't explain why she felt so comfortable with him. They toured the zoo and the aquarium.

'Pity that you're due to leave. You'd enjoy whale-watching.'

Amy didn't want to think about leaving. 'Will you have to change tactics if that man starts to haggle?'

He shrugged. 'No; we've made him a fair offer.'

'The Blue Boar is okay for a beer but it's very basic, isn't it? Where will visitors stay?'

'We're building some self-catering cabins. They should be ready in a few weeks' time. Some people in the town are willing to take in paying guests, and if tourism takes off, we'll consider building a small hotel.'

'Sounds exciting.'

Happiness already filled her but, when he leaned forward, her breath caught in her throat and she swallowed hard as she stared at his face. She felt the heat of his body and her heart pounded erratically as his hands cupped her face. He brushed a gentle kiss across her forehead and then his mouth took possession of her lips and his kiss grew more demanding. She was lost, despite all well-meant intentions. Putting one of his hands round her waist, he drew her closer. She seemed to stop breathing and could feel the thudding of his heart. There was a need for him crawling around inside as his hand moved gently down her back. Her brain told her heart it was madness. She lived on the opposite side of the Atlantic.

She breathed heavily between parted lips and he kissed her slowly again. She was powerless and felt a hunger that she couldn't hide. Her body ached for his touch and she was shocked at her own eagerness. He pulled away for a brief moment and ran a finger gently down the side of her cheek, before he kissed the side of her jaw and she kissed him back.

They walked towards the south shore, towards a group of totem poles. She took a photo for a passing Japanese tourist, and he offered to take one of her and Luke. Luke pulled her close, and her heart thundered. They sat down on one of the nearby benches. Amy closed her eyes and stretched out her legs.

An attractive blonde-haired woman on a bike braked suddenly. 'I'll be damned. It's Luke. What are you doing here?'

Luke got up. 'Good heavens, I could ask you the same. Hi, Sue! I'm just visiting. How's George?'

She was evenly tanned and had a trim figure. 'Fine. He's out sailing.' She smiled and glanced in Amy's direction.

'Sue, this is Amy.' He explained, 'Sue was a fellow student.'

'Hello, Amy.'

Amy returned her smile. 'Hello.'

'What a coincidence. Hey, some of the crowd are coming round for drinks this evening. If you're not doing anything, join us.'

Luke laughed noncommittally.

'Oh, come on, Luke. We haven't seen you for ages.'

Amy hoped he realized he was free to go.

'Bring Amy.'

Luke hesitated. 'Perhaps, if Amy doesn't mind . . . '

'Know where we live?'

'Lawnton — or was it Lawrence Road?'

'Lawrence, number twenty-seven. Any time after seven, informal, no food — just tidbits and drinks. See you.' She pushed off, waving as she went.

When she was out of sight, he said, 'I can see them another time.'

'You ought to go.'

'I don't intend to ditch you for them. They weren't part of my plans.'

Amy wanted to say that she wasn't either, but she didn't. 'Then I'll come. She invited me too.'

He considered and nodded. 'Okay, we'll go to China Town for lunch instead of this evening.'

★ ★ ★

They went by taxi to a sprawling modern house built on an incline overlooking the harbour. The windows were ablaze with light. Inside, a man with a bear-like stature thumped Luke's back. 'You son of a gun. We haven't met since Walt Freeman's wedding.' He pumped Luke's hand up and down and then noticed Amy. 'Oh, forgive me, you're . . . ?'

'Amy, Amy Watson.'

He shook her hand. 'Quite a fluke, Sue meeting you this morning. Go through; she's in there somewhere.'

They found Sue, balancing tidbits and fighting her way through the throng. 'Hi. I'm glad you made it.

Follow me; the others are in the kitchen.'

There was a lot of back thumping when they joined a group standing in Sue's ultra-modern white kitchen. Luke tried to introduce Amy, but the ensuing remarks were all madcap ones, and Luke gave up. The conversation soon revolved around their university days.

Sue caught Amy's arm. 'This must be boring for you. Come and have a look around the house.' Amy followed.

The house was expensive, select, sophisticated like something out of a glossy magazine, but it lacked warmth. Amy couldn't imagine that it was a place for children to play.

'It's lovely. Do you have children?'

Sue shook her head. 'I'm a career person; we don't plan to have children. I don't want the hassle of diapers, baby food, and schools. I don't have strong maternal instincts. I suppose you think that sounds very self-centred?'

Amy shook her head. 'It's entirely up to you and your husband.'

Sue paused. 'But you think differently?'

'I like children. It's not always an easy decision, is it? When a woman has invested time and effort in education and climbing the career ladder, it's hard to slam on the brakes just because of children.'

'Most women have a biological clock; I don't.'

Amy laughed. 'It's no one else's business.'

'What do you do?'

'I'm starting a new job with a firm of UK publishers soon.'

'So you're on vacation?'

Amy nodded. 'With relatives in Pineville; that's where I met Luke.'

'You must meet Julian. He owns a publishing business in Montreal. He's rich, talented and thrice married.'

Sue left her with Julian; Amy enjoyed talking shop. He was in his late thirties with a lively face and eyes framed by rimless glasses.

'You came with Luke?'

'Yes, do you know him?'

'I'm distantly related. My first wife was one of Luke's friends.' Julian took another sip of cognac. 'Luke was popular with the girls, but as far as I remember he only ever had one serious one.'

'Stop telling tales, Julian.' Luke reappeared at her side.

'Just informing Amy about things she should know.'

Luke placed his arm proprietorially round her shoulder. The two men chatted until George dragged Julian away to help him refill glasses.

There was a hint of disapproval in Luke's voice. 'Julian's okay . . . in small doses.'

'Sue said he's been married three times. I'm trying to figure out why women find him so fascinating.'

'Money! He made money fast, and that attracts some women like bears to honey.'

'If that's why, I'm sorry for him.'

'Well I'm not. Anyone can make a

mistake once, but three times? I don't understand why he bothers to get married when he realises he's not marriage material.' He shrugged. 'Perhaps the women just want to make certain they'll get a generous divorce settlement.'

They went back to the kitchen. Teasing, someone said, 'Afraid someone will pinch her?'

'Spot on.'

She listened and joined the conversation when she could, but then Luke gradually pulled her out of the circle. She didn't resist. They found Sue and George and thanked them.

'Where can we get a taxi?' asked Luke.

'There's a number next to the phone,' Sue replied.

The sky was a blanket of black velvet splattered with silver stars. Amy reflected that being with Luke in the taxi meant more to her than all the rest of the evening. She said, 'I like your friends. They're nice.'

He shrugged. 'I suppose so. I don't see them often anymore. My priorities have changed. I used to be a townie, but I now find town life very artificial.'

As their eyes met in the darkness she felt her heartbeat rocketing. 'You lived and worked in Vancouver after university, didn't you?'

'Yes, for a couple of years. At that time all I wanted from life was an opulent office in the financial district, an exclusive bungalow overlooking the inlet and plenty of cash in the bank.'

'And things changed overnight?'

He looked ahead. 'Not overnight. I just decided to do something for Pineville and have time for other interests.'

'And you moved back. Do you regret it?'

'Not at all. I get real satisfaction running the businesses and involving myself in community issues. It's challenging and rewarding.' He smiled. 'You can make money in small towns like Pineville; not huge amounts, but enough. I'm happier with my lifestyle now; it's quieter and the surroundings are perfect. In a city you're anonymous; in

Pineville you can't buy a headache tablet without someone suggesting you visit Doc Hampton.'

She laughed softly in agreement. 'People in Pineville are grateful that you've created new jobs.'

He nodded. 'I know. Life doesn't always need to be in the fast lane. Look at Sue and George. George works like crazy and spends every free minute sailing, hunting or playing badminton. Sue has rocketed upwards but doesn't want children. They have oodles of money but they live in an empty shell. I often wonder what keeps them together and why they married in the first place.'

She shrugged. 'They seem satisfied. That kind of life wouldn't suit me either, but it takes all kinds to make a world.'

His gaze was riveted on her face. 'What would suit you?'

The pit of her stomach tingled. 'Oh, very down-to-earth things. An interesting job, a good marriage, children one day, and time to enjoy life.'

He gazed outside. 'Have you anyone

special waiting at home?'

She looked across. 'No. It's not easy to find the right person, is it? It's better to stay single than end up with the wrong partner.'

He agreed in soft tones. 'You're right there.'

When they reached the hotel, he paid the taxi and said, 'What about a nightcap?'

17

Amy was delighted; it would lengthen their time together.

He tucked his hand under her elbow as they crossed the reception area, heading towards the hotel bar. Piano music wafted towards them as he unbuttoned his jacket, loosened his tie, and guided them towards the break in the dividing partition.

Amy stopped abruptly when she saw Jill hurrying out of the lift and coming towards them, and too shocked to notice the expression on Luke's face or his reactions. She did feel how the colour left her face as Jill rushed towards them, an artificial smile cutting her face in two. When she reached them, she stood on tiptoe and kissed Luke on his cheek.

The relaxed mood had disappeared. He regarded Jill with curiosity, but Amy was too busy looking at the floor to notice. He said, 'Jill. What a surprise.'

'I found that I needed to come to Vancouver too, after you left. I anticipated us spending time together. I see you already have a substitute.'

Too polite to correct her formulation, he remained silent and didn't answer.

Jill's laugh tinkled and she gave Amy a glance. 'I didn't expect you'd be spending time with Amy.'

'Why not?'

There was a moment of awkward silence. Amy didn't know what to say. A tumble of confused thoughts assailed her. Jill waited, unaffected by the atmosphere. Luke stood silently and Amy felt embarrassed. She had nothing to be embarrassed about, but she couldn't dismiss the idea that perhaps Luke and Jill had intended to meet but something had come in between, and she was just Luke's last-minute replacement. Jill would now be included in the last few hours of their stay, and Amy didn't like the idea.

She was too concerned about herself to note Luke's reactions. She lifted her chin and forced her lips into a curved, stiff smile. Facing him, she held out her hand. 'Thanks, Luke, for a really nice day. It was a pleasure to meet your friends.' With her heart pounding, she managed to add, 'Thanks for the whole weekend.'

'My pleasure.' His voice was cold. There was no return to the emotional heights of a moment ago; they both knew that.

He took her hand and Amy wanted to jerk it away, but she let it rest for a moment until Jill thrust her arm through his, saying, 'We can have a nightcap and talk about what I've missed before we go to bed.'

Luke opened his mouth to say something but Jill wrenched at his elbow and drew him towards the bar. Over her shoulder she added half-heartedly, knowing that Amy would refuse, 'What about you?'

Amy shook her head. 'No, thanks.'

Luke looked back and forth between the two of them. Amy turned and walked away towards the open lift. As the doors closed, she thought he was trying to hide his annoyance. His expression was bland but his eyes were fierce.

Later her telephone rang, several times. She ignored it. It could only be Luke and she didn't want to listen to explanations. She'd never wanted a man so much before, but why open Pandora's box? She'd soon be thousands of kilometres away. They had no future.

She gulped and felt utterly miserable. She managed to hold back the tears of disappointment for a moment, looked at her white face in the mirror, and finally burst into tears.

18

Next morning Amy thought about dispensing with breakfast, but she wasn't a coward. She wasn't sure if she was sorry, or relieved, to find that Luke wasn't there. Jill was, and she patted a neighbouring seat.

Amy hoped she looked calmer than she felt. 'Morning.'

Jill put her newspaper aside and picked up a piece of dry toast. 'Luke has already left. Some man or other wanted to talk to him about this winter tourism business before he left this morning.' She patted the corner of her mouth with a serviette.

Amy nodded. 'I'll get some juice. Want some?'

'No, thanks. I've got what I need.'

Amy returned to the table and Jill pushed the plate with the remains of her toast aside. 'I'm waiting for Luke.

We'll travel back together.'

Amy nodded. If she'd cared less, it wouldn't have mattered so much. She cleared her throat. 'I'm catching the bus. Ruth is expecting me.'

Jill checked her watch. 'You'll have to hurry! It leaves in half an hour and there's only this one today.'

'I know. I've already packed and checked out.'

'Of course.' She stood up. 'Well, I'm off to empty the shops until Luke calls me. See you.' If eyes were the mirrors of one's soul, at this moment Jill's were made of solid ice. She strode towards the door and didn't look back. Amy finished breakfast, picked up her bag and set off for the bus station.

Once she was in the bus Amy had time to think. She was now certain that she loved Luke, even though they had no future. She'd met the one man in her life she wanted, but it was the wrong place and time. She hid in the corner of the back seat, staring unseeingly out of the bus, and didn't register much about the journey until they were nearing Pineville. The bus had to stop to let a wide transporter pass. They were opposite the overgrown trail Luke had driven down towards the paint factory.

She could see there was a large van parked a little way down the track and another car beyond that. It was easy to pick them out from the bus. Amy came to life, grabbed her camera from the front pocket of her backpack and took a couple of photos of the van and the company name before the bus sped on again. A plan to help Luke formed in her head, and she had to figure out how to achieve it.

She was home in plenty of time to make a meal for Ruth and Alan. When they arrived she tried to sound enthusiastic when she told them about Vancouver, about the hotel and about meeting Luke and Jill. Ruth gave her a searching look but didn't comment.

★　★　★

Next morning she went to the local drugstore and bought some cheap economy-size plastic bottles for storing cosmetics. She transferred the pictures from her camera onto her computer without checking them, reloaded the camera's battery, and then inserted a brand new storage card.

That evening when Alan came home from work, Amy asked, 'Can I borrow the car? I want to take some photos of the campground and the surroundings.'

He threw the keys on to the table. 'Of course.'

Amy picked them up. 'I won't be long.' He nodded.

She grabbed her backpack and drove out to the old paint factory. The track was free and there was no one else around. Some birds sang in the undergrowth, but apart from that she only heard her own footsteps flattening twigs and the rough grasses. The undergrowth near the gateway was newly trampled and flattened, but there wasn't much difference to when she'd been here with Luke. Then she noticed that some of the rusty barrels alongside the nearest building had disappeared. Were they already trying to clear any superficial damage before the authorities got involved?

The wire netting looked formidable, but she had to find out what was going on, for Luke's sake. That and her journalistic curiosity triumphed. She shoved her camera into the backpack, checked that she had everything she needed, and hoisted it onto her shoulders. She took a flying jump at the fence and, snatching at the wiring, she grappled her way to the top. The fence was roughly two and a half meters high and she lowered herself by clambering down the other side. She landed safely and crept towards the buildings with their broken windows.

The wind came up and the corrugated iron roofs rattled. It wasn't difficult to get inside. Someone had been collecting various barrels and stacking them there to hide them from immediate view, or just to get them ready for transport. They stood in forlorn groups and there were similar ones in the other sheds and buildings. Amy got to work, taking photos of the buildings and the barrels. She took photos inside any open doors or windows, and anything else outside that looked suspicious, including the faded labels on some of the barrels with their toxic hazard signs.

Daylight was fading when she began to take samples of what she thought were contaminated areas. She measured the distance from noticeable points to the contaminated spots and noted the details about their position as best she could in a notepad as she went along. She gave the sample bottles and the area the same number by scribbling numbers hastily on bits of paper and placing the numbered samples next to them before she took the photos. The wind in the trees and the remote location made her nervous, and she didn't know if the hidden camera under the roof was functioning or not, but she was determined to get as much detail as she could.

She hurried but it all took longer than she expected. When the light began to fade, she took a couple of general photos of the layout of the various buildings from the top of the fence on her way out. She'd done what she could to help Luke, and was glad to leave. He was right; the ground was completely contaminated.

★　★　★

Next morning, Amy needed some cash so she went into the bank. Luke was standing next to the manager, and Amy thought about bolting because she still felt uncomfortable about meeting Jill in Vancouver. He looked at her and smiled, then came across.

'You got back safely then? I wish you hadn't disappeared, and had come to the hotel bar with us. It would have made things a lot easier for me.'

She tried to throttle the dizzying currents in her heart. 'How did your meeting go?'

'It went well. You know Ben?' The bank manager was studying the papers in his hands impatiently. Amy nodded at him, although Ben didn't notice. 'We have to put a financial proposal together, and then I have to take it to Montreal.'

She nodded. 'Hope it all works out. I won't keep you; you're obviously busy.'

Luke said, 'Look, Amy, I need to explain about why Jill turned up like that. I don't want you to get the wrong impression. I'm in a bit of a hurry now, but as soon as I get back I'll be in touch.'

She swallowed hard and hoped she sounded calm. 'There's nothing for you to explain. You're not beholden to tell me anything. Don't worry about it. Have a good journey, and good luck!' She smiled and turned away. When she looked back, the manager was hurrying Luke towards the inner office, talking energetically on the way.

Amy was glad that they'd met and that they still seemed to be friends. She only wished she'd been able to show him the photos and tell him about what she'd found at the factory. She couldn't tell him anything in front of a stranger, so it would have to wait.

19

When Amy left the bank, she walked to the newsagent's further down the street. The air was sharper and winter was on the way. Sunlight was still strong during the day, but the cold nights were changing the colour of some of the leafed trees. She'd even felt a flurry of snowflakes recently. She chatted to the woman in the shop and headed home. Then she saw Jill coming towards her, and she wished there was some way she could avoid her.

'Amy. Have you a moment to spare?'

'I haven't, actually. I'm meeting someone in ten minutes. Any special reason?'

'Ten minutes will be plenty of time. Just a chat. Let's have a coffee.'

Amy was obliged to follow her into the town's only coffee bar.

'Grab a table. I'll get some coffees.'

When she returned she asked, 'How are things? Good journey home?'

'Fine, thanks.' She made an effort not to show animosity. 'And you?'

'Couldn't be better.'

Amy waited. Jill's features were benign but her eyes were malignant. 'I thought I should warn you not to build up hopes about Luke. You can't control men, however much you love them. He's had girlfriends on the side in the past, and will have others in the future. I accept that.'

The colour left Amy's face. She gripped her mug tightly with both hands. 'What has that to do with me?'

Jill stirred her coffee vigorously. 'After I saw you together in Vancouver, I thought a quiet word of warning wouldn't go amiss.' Amy's brain was frozen as she viewed her. Jill gave her a sheepish smile. 'We women are very foolish sometimes when it comes to men, aren't we? Luke always thinks he's entitled to take what he wants with no strings attached — especially when it is being offered on a silver plate.'

Amy was alert again and fumed. 'And exactly why are you warning me?' Amy had the satisfaction of seeing Jill redden. 'I'm not pursuing Luke. And I'm not offering him anything on a silver plate. I'm flying home soon. This conversation is entirely superfluous.'

Jill's face brightened visibly. 'Really? I didn't realise that. I thought you might be hurt when you heard that Luke and I are . . . '

Amy got up and left without another word. She was too much in love with Luke to stay and listen. She didn't belong here. She didn't need to listen to Jill warning her to stay away from Luke.

She knew Luke didn't want a serious relationship. Judy had told her so. She knew in recent years his girlfriends had been fleeting and temporary ones. If he manoeuvred her into accepting an affair, Amy was well aware it could only be a passing one. She didn't intend to act stupidly. She'd leave. Jill was welcome to him. Perhaps Jill was satisfied with whatever he was prepared to give, even if it led nowhere in the end. Amy wasn't. She found it hard to believe he was a philanderer, but Jill's words on top of what Judy had told her made her wary. She wouldn't act recklessly for the mere reward of an irresponsible brief fling.

Feeling disillusioned, Amy made up her mind to end it all and marched determinedly to the local travel agent. She felt slightly better when she'd made a provisional booking in three days' time and told the woman, 'I'll bring my ticket in tomorrow so that you can fill in the details.'

Back at Ruth's, she decided to organise the photos and samples from the paint factory for Luke. She explained what she'd found, how she'd collected and classified the samples with the corresponding photos, and put it all into a parcel.

When she finished, curiosity started her off surfing the internet. She decided to invest some spare time in finding the present owner of the paint factory. She found out by entering the name on the side of the van that she'd seen the morning she returned from Vancouver on the bus. It led her to Sullivan Industries. Sullivan had bought it from the original owners for chickenfeed in the late seventies, thinking it was on to a bargain. It was never reopened because stricter ecological regulations were on the way. That made it a dead duck as far as Sullivan was concerned, and any attempts at selling it to someone else later must have been unsuccessful. People didn't want the expensive responsibility of clearing the site before they could utilise it for something else. No wonder Luke had stirred up a hornet's nest when he started his protests. Amy also recalled that Sullivan was the name of his former girlfriend. She checked Sullivan's website. It displayed a picture of the top management and Amy was absolutely shocked to find Jill's picture among them. She was listed as

'Development Engineer — In Charge of Research Projects'.

Staring at Jill's picture in a spotless lab coat, Amy felt her anger growing. She entered 'Ecosystems Canada' and found nothing. There was no such organisation. That meant Sullivan had presumably sent Jill to spy on Luke. Amy stared at the screen and thought about what she should do. She decided to give him the initial information about seeing the name on the side of the van and leave the rest up to him. He might be so much in love with Jill that he'd want to forgive and forget. She printed out what she'd found about Sullivan owning the factory, without any further comment, then put the information on top of everything else in the parcel.

When they came home, she told Ruth and Alan she was leaving on the weekend. They immediately protested and said there was plenty of time yet.

She shook her head. 'You know that I still have to find somewhere to live.'

'We've loved having you; you'll come back soon?'

Amy took Ruth by the shoulders and gave her a quick hug. 'You've been wonderful. I've had a great time and I'll never forget that. You have to visit us first.'

When she went to say goodbye to Rod, they talked about various things for a while. He noticed her nervousness and her expression tensed markedly as soon as he mentioned Luke and his trip to Montreal. Was Luke so stupid? Was he prepared to just let her go? He wouldn't be back before she left. Rod eyed her and knew it was none of his business. He decided not to press her for information, but he could tell something was very wrong.

In some ways Amy wished she could have handed the parcel over to Luke personally, but it was better that she didn't see him anymore. She loved him too much. She went to say cheerio to Judy and Don, taking the parcel with her.

Judy was startled. 'I was expecting to hear about Vancouver, not that you're leaving.'

Amy smiled and handed Judy her perfume. 'I have to find a flat or some rooms before I start my job.'

Judy nodded. 'Okay! But I'll miss you.'

'I'll miss you too. I'll write, promise.'

'Luke said you met up in Vancouver. Does he know you're leaving? He's in Montreal.'

'Yes, that's right. I didn't have the chance to tell him I was leaving. He was busy and so was I.' She cleared her throat. She handed Judy the parcel. 'Please give him this when he gets back; it's very important. Say goodbye from me, and thank him for his kindness and for showing me Vancouver.'

Judy was frustrated. 'I was going to ask you to be Claire's godmother and planned to have the christening before you left. I didn't expect you to leave so abruptly.'

She smiled. 'That's one of the nicest

compliments I've ever had, but it's not practical, is it? Not with me living in the UK. I may never come back.'

'Whyever not? I thought you liked Pineville?'

'I did, I do . . . but life goes on, and you know how it is.' She squirmed. 'Come and visit me; I'll show you around a couple of proper museums.' Judy chuckled. Amy couldn't believe that she'd never see Tim again; he'd won a special place in her heart. Amy found it hard to say goodbye to them all. Judy kissed her on the cheek before she left.

'Look after your family, and look after yourself, Judy.'

Don kissed her cheek and she hugged Tim and promised to send him postcards of soldiers. She felt tearful.

* * *

Amy was kept busy with saying goodbye to people and packing. She tried not to think about Luke. At least no one, apart from Jill, suspected she loved him. Her pride was still intact. She was thankful she'd be able to bundle her energies into her new job; it would stop her thinking about Luke.

Alan and Ruth drove her to the airport.

20

Amy phoned Ruth as soon as she was home, to tell her she'd arrived safely.

She thought time would help, and she'd learn how to forget Luke, but she didn't. Every week seemed to drag, and life didn't have much rhyme or reason anymore. She'd never felt so miserable.

She hoped she'd be able to tell her parents about him one day; her mother sensed something was amiss. She wasn't even able to talk about him to her best friend. It hurt too much to think that perhaps he'd forgiven Jill and they were now a steady pair with plans for the future. In contrast, Amy was starting a new job in a new town. Her family and old friends would be far away.

After several days of intensive hunting, Amy gave up looking for an empty flat and took a small ready-furnished one, close to her new job. She reasoned she'd have time to look for something permanent once she'd completed her trial period and settled down. She wasn't sleeping well, and dreamt about Luke when she did. The last weekend before starting her new job, she came home to collect some bits and pieces to make her rooms look more comfy.

Ruth had sent a note and a copy of the *Gazette*. Amy's mother pointed. 'There's another letter from Canada, behind the clock.'

Amy slit the envelope and read quickly. Her eyes brightened. 'It's from Judy Harrison. How nice of her to write so soon.' The letter was full of anecdotes about Tim and Claire. She also mentioned Luke was back from Montreal and she'd given him Amy's parcel straight away. It had whipped him into immediate action, and he was also extremely busy with the run-up to the opening of the ski lift. It looked like he had Sullivan Industries by the throat at last. Amy read through to the end.

She looked up and said, 'She still wants me to be Claire's godmother. It's such an unrealistic idea.'

Her mother nodded. Looking at her, she could tell something was troubling Amy. She wondered what it was. She hadn't talked much about Canada since she came back. 'Yes, it would be difficult, you living here, but it all depends how seriously you intend to take your responsibilities. I think godparents should keep an eye on their godchildren, but nowadays that doesn't always apply.'

'I'll have to write and tell her again to find someone else.' Amy put the letter away. 'I need some fresh air. I'm going for a walk. Need anything?'

* * *

Her new work was interesting. The company specialized in non-fiction literature and had a small staff. Amy's colleagues were helpful and friendly. She soon struck up a friendship with one girl in particular. They went out for meals, to the cinema and did various other things together. That helped, but there wasn't a day she didn't think about Luke. Time and distance didn't make any difference. She decided to get the photos she'd taken in Canada printed. It was a delight to see the town and all the people. It ached like crazy when she saw the pictures of Luke and her together.

Christmas was getting closer. The shops and window displays were full of suggestions and enticing presents. Christmas songs and traditional carols filled the ears of people shopping and on radio programmes. All they needed now was snow, but most days Amy battled her way through the wind and rain. Next time she went home on the weekend her mother was already planning the Christmas menu.

'There's another letter from Canada. It arrived at the beginning of last week.'

Amy didn't recognize the bold writing at first, but then her heart began to race. She ripped it open quickly.

Dear Amy,

I wish you'd waited a day or two longer. It was a bit of a shock to come back and find you'd left.

I'm extremely grateful for all the information you left about Sullivan's paint factory. You shouldn't have taken such a risk. It gave me all I needed to pin them down at last. Sullivan immediately put a team of lawyers to work, hoping to worm his way out, but the national newspapers picked it up (thanks to Rod) and he's now having a tough time of it. Hoorah!

Judy is quite determined that you'll be Claire's godmother. You know the Harrison family is stubborn once they've made up their minds, so please do think about coming back. We want to see you again.

It's snowing regularly now. Everyone is busy keeping his driveway clear. I'm glad I bought one of those snow sweepers — otherwise I'd be spending every free moment digging my way out.

I hope you are well, that you like your new job, and that you'll think very seriously about being Claire's godmother.

Take care of yourself,
Yours,
Luke

She folded it and shoved it quickly into the pocket of her trousers. 'It's from Luke, Judy's brother.' Trying to sound nonchalant, she added, 'Just some news about Pineville and that I should think again about being Claire's godmother.'

Amy's mother noticed how the colour had suddenly brightened her cheeks. She wondered how long she could prevent herself from asking questions.

Amy read the letter, in secret, numerous times over the weekend. It was something to hold onto. She noted he hadn't mentioned Jill. Did that mean she wasn't around anymore, or that perhaps he was too embarrassed to mention her part in the fraud?

Back in Bath, she decided it was time to send cards to everyone, and she could include any photos she'd promised. She could send Luke the photos together with her Christmas card and include a short letter. Amy steamed ahead. She had the photos developed, bought a pile of Christmas cards and thought very carefully about what to write to him.

Dear Luke,

Thank you for your letter. I'm glad if I helped to nail Sullivan's.

I started my new job a few weeks ago. The work is interesting and my colleagues are all nice and very patient. I'm gradually settling down, and trying to make new friends again.

I promised copies of the photos — well, here they are.

It rains here every day. I'm seriously thinking of buying a pair of wellingtons — and I live just down the road from our offices. The skies are grey, the wind is blustery and *nature is asleep. Your description of all the snow makes me envious.*

I'm very flattered that Judy thinks I'd make a suitable godmother for Claire, but it's not a very practical idea, is it? I'm sure there's someone in her circle of friends who lives 'on the spot', and would be a perfect godmother.

I hope that you're well, and wish you every success with your winter tourism and everything else you plan for the future. Thank you for all your kindness during my stay. I'll never forget Pineville and all the people I met there. A Very Merry Xmas and a Happy New Year.

Best wishes,
Amy.

She posted all the cards for Canada at the same time. The envelopes fell with a thud into the box and a weight lifted from her heart. In a couple of weeks' time, when she was certain she'd need no more copies, she'd delete the photos from her computer. Perhaps that would help her to forget.

When she went home the following week, Ruth phoned. She spoke to Amy's mother, and then to Amy. 'I met Judy yesterday, and she asked me again to persuade you to be Claire's godmother. Luke came into the shop too. I can't remember him doing so before. He told me that Judy is keeping on and asked me to tell you to think about it seriously. Can't you come?'

'I'm not entitled to any holidays yet. I don't want to leave Mum and Dad alone at Christmas.'

'You won't. Your mum just told me that Nick and his family are coming down. A christening is so special, and Judy is so determined. Try to make it, Amy! If you don't come now, it sounds like she'll only put it off until later when you can. She's determined about it.'

Amy sat staring unseeingly at a book and thinking about the phone call.

Her mother could stand it no more. 'Amy, love, what's wrong? What's bothering you? Is it something to do with work?'

'No, work is fine, and the people are nice.'

'You've been down in the dumps since you got back from Canada. And then all these letters and phone calls . . . '

Amy had a lump in her throat. 'Sorry. I didn't want to worry you. I'm in a fix. I met someone in Canada and fell hook, line and sinker for him.'

There was a moment of astonishment in her mother's face, but then she said, 'And where's the problem? Does Ruth know him?'

'Yes.'

'Come on . . . tell me about him. What's his name? What's he like?'

'Luke Thornton. He's great — all I ever hoped for. He liked me. I've tried to forget him, but I can't.'

'And how does he feel?'

'I wasn't brave enough to find out exactly before I left.'

'Why not? If you liked each other,

what was in the way?'

'I'm not sure if he's the type for a serious relationship. He may have another girlfriend. And his life is in Canada, mine is here.'

She looked at Amy. 'If you love him, it wouldn't make any difference if he lived on the moon; you'll still want to be with him.'

'Even if I had the chance, I couldn't leave Dad and you, all the things I know and love.'

'You could and you would, if it's the love of a lifetime. Don't think about us. We moved away from our families when we married. It didn't break the ties we had. We only want you to be happy. If your destiny is in Canada, we'll cope with that. Canada isn't on Mars.' She laughed softly. 'It's wonderful that you put us first in your plans, but you must lead your own life. I don't think that Canada is the problem. Your problem is that you are scared to find out the truth about this man, isn't it?'

Amy was surprised that her mother

was so philosophical, but her spirits lifted as she thought about what that meant. She ought to see him again and find out if he did love her, or perhaps that he'd forgiven Jill and loved her instead.

★　★　★

She hadn't been in the company long, but when Amy explained she'd been asked to be a godmother to someone in Canada her boss gave her ten unpaid days off. She wrote to Judy telling her she was trying to get a flight. The airlines were booked up, but two weeks beforehand, someone cancelled. Amy emailed Judy and gave her the go-ahead. Judy answered that she was delighted.

Amy bought a christening present and Christmas presents for Ruth and Alan and Tim. She borrowed a ski-overall from a friend and packed some warm sweaters.

21

Amy couldn't believe she was back. She looked out of Alan's car at familiar and yet strange-looking surroundings because everything was covered in snow. On arrival, Pineville basked in sunshine. It was a winter wonderland. To keep the traffic moving, a snow plough was making one of its frequent clearances of the main street. Fir trees bowed under a mantel of white and the mountaintops were completely hidden beneath caps of snow. The roofs everywhere were layered deep in snow, and the neat gardens were camouflaged and covered by wind-driven piles of white flurries.

She was tired after the non-stop flight and the drive to Pineville, but she phoned Judy to tell her she'd arrived.

'If you're not too tired, come up and we'll tell you about tomorrow.'

Amy didn't think twice even if she

was tired; she wanted to see them. She donned her ski-overall and tramped up to Judy's cabin. The snow crackled and crunched under her feet. Don's jeep and another car were outside. Her knock brought Judy to the door, and Amy was enveloped in a hug. Inside, a delicious smell of baking wafted through the rooms. Tim came whizzing down the corridor and she bent down to pick him up and swing him around. Don's parents had come for the christening, and were staying for Christmas.

Judy told her how the national press had landed like a ton of bricks on Sullivan Industries. It emerged, as Amy suspected, that they'd sent Jill under false pretences and with the aim of silencing local resistance. It didn't make good publicity. Amy listened and finished her mug of coffee laced with cognac without comments or any questions.

Judy smiled. 'We're so glad you came, and don't begrudge you an early night. We'll have a proper chat when the christening is over.'

Amy walked home through the sharp cold air. Some muffled figures passed her on the road but she met no one she knew. She checked the newspaper office, but it was in darkness.

Ruth and Alan packed her off to bed and she was asleep in seconds.

★　★　★

Early next morning she stretched contentedly. Sunbeams spilled through the windows onto her bedcovers. Amy thought how fantastic the snow-covered peaks of the distant mountains looked. She studied them from her warm cocoon and was glad she had plenty of time to get ready.

She'd hunted through the shops for the right trouser-suit for the christening. The short green jacket highlighted her slender waist, and the narrow trousers flattered her long legs and slim hips. Amy shoved Claire's christening present into her bag and joined Alan and Ruth to pile into Alan's jeep and drive to church. She reassured herself that she only needed to actually see Luke again, and then she'd be able to calm down.

Her breath caught in her throat when she saw him. When their eyes met, Amy's heart began to hammer out of control. She forced her lips into a smile, and mouthed a silent 'Hello' before she sat down in a seat near the altar. The ceremony went off without a hitch. Amy even forgot Luke for a minute as she concentrated on her part in the simple but moving ceremony. Claire behaved beautifully. Back at the homestead, Don welcomed everyone, and they toasted Claire's future health and happiness.

Amy wasn't quite strong enough to confront Luke. She chatted nervously to Don's father. Then Luke joined them, and Amy's fingers grasped her glass more tightly. He stood, a silent observer, until Don called him to help with the drinks. Later, he followed her into the kitchen, and she couldn't avoid him any longer.

'How was the flight?'

He looked wonderful; he was still the only man she'd ever want. With a lump in her throat, she tried to sound sensible. 'Fine . . . I see that the ski-lift is functioning. I went to look this morning, before church.'

He rubbed his hand over his mouth and chin. 'Yes, it is. We have to talk . . .'

Her mouth was dry and her mind froze. Then Judy shouted. 'Amy, can you bring me the serviettes from the breakfast bar?' Amy rushed to comply. She needed time to adjust to the fact that Luke was within reach again first.

In the crush of people coming and going, Luke offered to drive some people home, and Amy decided to leave too. She asked Judy, 'Can I help you tidy up before I go?'

'No, my mother-in-law will help. I will be grateful for help tomorrow though.'

'Doing what?'

'Luke is having a party tomorrow evening. He's ordered the food from a caterer, but wants me to add some extra decorations. If you help, I'll be finished in half the time.'

Amy tried to think of an excuse. Nothing came to mind. She was here to find out how he felt; perhaps this was her chance. She would be prepared for him next time they met. She hoped she would be able to tell if he only wanted her friendship, before she said something stupid. She didn't want to make a fool of herself. She smiled weakly. 'Of course. What time?'

'About ten?'

Amy nodded.

*　*　*

She slept badly. Alan had already left when she came down to breakfast. Ruth explained, 'He's gone to chop down our Christmas tree with some of his friends. Will you bring me milk on the way back?'

'Of course.'

'Betty is open all day.'

'I won't be long. I expect Judy has

everything planned and organized.' She glanced out of the window. 'It's a lovely morning. This is a picture-book Christmas Eve. I'd better go, or I'll be late.'

'When you get back, you can help us decorate the tree. I'm just going down to the cellar to dig out the boxes of ornaments from the pile of stuff down there.'

Main Street was busy. The snow sparkled like diamonds and crackled under Amy's feet. She walked along the tracks made by the wheels to go up the hill so that she didn't need to plough through the thick drifts of snow.

By the time she reached Luke's cabin, her cheeks glowed. It was gone ten. Misty grey smoke curled lazily out of the chimney stack. Sunlight glistened on the snow. Amy climbed the steps with her heart pounding.

22

She knocked and waited. Her heart beat faster and faster. The door flew open and she faced him. It took a fraction of a second before she found her voice and broke the silence. 'Hullo, Luke!' Her voice faded. She was tongue-tied and riveted to the spot.

'Good, you've come. Come in!'

She tried to smile, but her lips were stiff. Luke almost pulled her inside. 'Take your boots off.'

Amy noted that despite all her efforts to remain calm, he had exactly the same effect on her as he did before she left, weeks ago. The interim period was swept away by a single glance. He turned her bones to liquid and her longing for him soared. The square cheekbones, black curly hair, and sensual mouth sent her senses spinning. Amy followed him into the living room.

Logs were crackling in the fireplace.

'Where's Judy?' Amy asked. 'Is she . . . ?' The question remained unanswered because he'd disappeared down the corridor. She struggled out of her ski-overall and waited, looking around the room. There were expensive leather settees, occasional tables with bulky lamps, and bookshelves that overflowed. Panorama windows looked out on snow-clad mountains and dark forests. A brilliant large fir tree decorated with plump red balls stood majestically next to the window, and Christmas cards hung on a crimson ribbon down the side of the fireplace. There were lots of others on the mantelpiece and Amy's heart skipped a beat when she noticed her card was dead centre. She told herself it didn't mean anything.

Luke returned with his eyebrows arched; he handed her a pair of thick stretch socks. 'Try these.'

She took them, and was glad to avoid his eyes for a moment. The socks were much too big, but she said, 'They're fine.' She straightened up and tried to control her voice. 'Do you know what Judy wanted to do? I can make a start.'

He said dryly, 'Judy's not coming.' He ignored her expression. 'I'm having a party this evening, that's true, but I don't need help. I just asked Judy to get you to come here this morning.'

Amy swallowed a lump in her throat.

'We need to talk, without interruption, don't we?'

She felt a moment of panic. Finding out how he felt about her wasn't as easy as she thought it would be. She looked at her ski-suit.

He followed her eyes. 'Oh no, don't even think about it. You're not running off again; not until we've sorted things.'

Her composure was fragile, but she had to face him because she had to hear the truth.

'Firstly, I have to say your excursion to the old paint works was daring and plucky, but also very risky. Did you tell anyone where you were going at the time?' She shook her head. He sounded exasperated. 'I thought so. Didn't you consider that someone might have been watching? One of Sullivan's henchmen? Someone could have knocked you around for breaking and entering. No one would have been there to help.' He reached out for her. 'Never, never, do anything so foolhardy again, promise me?'

Her throat was dry as she studied his face. She nodded silently. Luke pulled her to him. 'It was damned courageous, and I love you for it, but I'd have been half-crazy if I'd known what you were doing. I told you too much about that place and you seemed to think you needed to get involved. But thanks for all your investigation work. It soon linked Jill to Sullivan. I should've checked her out earlier, but she seemed so genuine. Why didn't you give me the information personally? Just a day or two longer and you would have had the chance to say goodbye to me too.'

Agitation swelled in her throat and

gnawed at her confidence. She clenched her hands and the colour in her face faded. 'I didn't need to be here for you to get the information. I just wanted to help. I asked Judy to say my goodbyes.'

'I was only worth a message through my sister? You said goodbye personally to Rod, to Mary at the library, to Betty at the bakery, Sam in the newsagent's. You cared more about all of them, than about me?'

Amy swallowed hard and moistened her lips. She found it hard to hold his glance. She noted his set face and fixed eyes. 'There was no offence intended. You just weren't here.'

'There's been something brewing between us for a long time — don't pretend you don't feel it too. The weekend in Vancouver made that very clear to me. It grew stronger each time we met, each time I saw you. At first I wondered if I was expecting too much; you were so cautious. I thought we had time to talk and be honest with each other when I got back from Montreal, but you bolted.'

Amy's insides were churned up but she spoke with quiet, desperate determination. 'I thought it was better to leave. Jill insinuated on several occasions that you and she were having an affair.'

His eyes widened in surprise. 'Rubbish! Did you honestly believe that? Did you think I'm a double-crossing cheat, and a liar?'

'No, but she kept hinting . . . '

His grey eyes were thunderclouds and tension was strong. 'You knew she was a fraud. You knew that she played a bogus role. Why should you believe a word of what she said? Why didn't you wait and ask me? I tried to get rid of her when she turned up in Vancouver that evening. I was angry about her interference. I phoned you to tell you so, and when you didn't answer, I left a letter at the desk. Did you get it?'

It was Amy's turn to look surprised. 'No. I left in a hurry, perhaps they forgot.'

He paused. 'Jill saw me handing it in. She guessed it was for you, and probably used your name to intercept it. The staff wouldn't remember what Amy Watson looked like.'

'What was in it?'

'Only that I was sorry about the way the day had finished, that I had to leave early, that I was looking forward to seeing you in Pineville, and that I'd told Jill to stay out of my private life in future. Back in Pineville, when we met in the bank, you were friendly and I thought everything was okay between us.'

He paused for a moment, looking thoughtful and annoyed. 'She realised that journalists are persistent nosy parkers and that we were too friendly for her peace of mind. You were threatening her success and she wanted you out of the way. Fate played into her hands because I had to go to Montreal. The longer you stayed, the greater the chance that you'd discover the truth about her and Sullivan's and pass it on to me.

Frightening you off and my absence gave her some more leeway to organize a clean-up. She didn't realise that you'd already been there, taking photos and samples. When I returned, I couldn't drop all the tourist preparations, handling Sullivan, and the opening of the ski-lift, although all I really wanted to do was follow you across the Atlantic.'

'When I read your letter,' she said, 'and you wrote about coming back for the christening, I couldn't tell if it was you who wanted to see me, or if you were just putting the pressure on for Judy's sake.'

He ran his hand through his hair. 'What do you think? Do you want me to be unhappy for the rest of my life?'

She took a deep breath and looked at him steadily. 'No, of course not. But I didn't know if you loved Jill enough to forgive her for spying on you like she did. My mother told me I should find out, face to face.'

He sighed contentedly. 'Your mother is a clever woman. I'm beginning to hope I'll hear what I've been longing to hear.' His arms slipped around her in a bear-like hug. Her face was buried in his chest and she breathed in the familiar sandalwood smell. They stared at each other before he bent his head and kissed her. His lips were warm and tender and a tide of passion raged through them both. Raising his mouth from hers a few seconds later, he said, 'I love you. And, I hope you're willing to give me a chance.'

She nodded and was free to admit, 'I love you too. I'll never belong to anyone else now.'

He exhaled in relief. 'If you don't want to live here, we'll find some other place to be together. I'll come to the UK, if you can't envisage moving here. I think women are more attached to places and people than men are.'

She reached up and slipped her hand round his neck. 'You've put so much work into your companies, and the town needs you, but I need you too. I like Pineville and I don't care really

where I am, as long as I'm with you.'
He beamed. She lifted her chin. 'I'll
need a job though; something to keep
me busy.'

He said emphatically, 'You're a
fantastic woman. You're prepared to
change your whole lifestyle for me. I
love you even more for that, if that's
possible.' He grinned. 'I'll find you
something safer than climbing over
rusty fences. The town is growing — I'll
be glad to unload some of my work
onto your shoulders if you like; give you
some sole responsibilities like handling
tourism, or running the hotel. That
would give me more time to take on
other things, and perhaps even dabble
in politics.'

Amy's eyes sparkled. His expression
was contemplative. 'If you want to stay
with journalism I'll buy up the majority
shares of the *Gazette*, and you can
modernise it, but I'm warning you — it
has to make a profit.'

She shook her head. 'That's not a
good idea. It's Rod's paper. It would be

264

unfair for me to push him out. I don't have the connections and feelings he has for the community. I'll be satisfied if you give me something that's equally rewarding.'

He kissed her. 'I want you more than I've ever wanted any other woman in the whole of my life before. I was busy pinning Sullivan's down for a while, and then fixing the opening of the ski-lift, but if you hadn't come to Claire's christening, I'd have been on the next flight out after Christmas to fight for you . . . to fight for us.'

Happiness was flowing and she felt euphoric. She buried her face in his neck and then kissed him. The mere touch of his hands made her tingle. She said, 'I can't imagine my life without you anymore.'

He crushed her to him and exhaled a sigh of contentment. 'And I know I've been waiting for you all my life. We haven't had enough time together, but I knew straight away that you were the one.' He picked her up and swung her round gently in sheer joy. 'I've been praying for this moment.'

She mused that Jill hadn't kept them apart, after all. 'How did Jill react when you confronted her?'

His eyes sparkled wickedly. 'She fell to pieces. She admitted that Sullivan told her to use any means to conceal his ownership. I could kick myself. I never thought about checking her out. She seemed so genuine and well-informed. She called too often for my liking. Including the day after we came back from the cabin. I can understand that you might have misunderstood that, but it didn't mean a thing. I now suspect she used the visits to make copies of my keys when I was out of the room. I think she was the one who burgled my office looking for information. I've had the locks changed everywhere since then.'

'If I ever see her again I'll kill her.'

He chuckled. 'Wow! I'd like to witness that, but she hasn't stopped running yet. Sullivan is an embittered, vengeful employer who won't forget.' He smiled and a devilish look sparkled in his eyes. 'Let's forget her; she's caused us nothing but trouble. Don't let her spoil today. Let's celebrate with some champagne.'

His arm firmly around her, he propelled her down the corridor to the kitchen. He took champagne from the icebox and filled two long-stemmed glasses, then touched her glass. 'Here's to us! Will you come? Will you marry me one day, when we know each other better?'

Her eyes were misty and wistful. 'Yes, Of course I'll come. Here's to us!' Amy took a sip.

He showed her the cabin. An enlarged version of them on the bench outside the museum in Vancouver stood on his bedside table. She picked it up. He watched her silently for a second before he said quietly, 'The looks on our faces kept my hopes alive. The longing for you hasn't stopped; it's gone on and on, and it'll never end.'

She stroked the side of his face; he turned his head slightly to kiss her fingers. Her pulse began to accelerate noticeably. He loved her. His eyes told her so; they were full of fire and devotion.

With evident emotion, he stated, 'Can we begin by picking up where we left off in Vancouver? We need to catch up on lost time.'

It seemed so right and natural to put her arms around his waist; she nodded silently.

He cradled her. 'How much time do we have?'

She came down to earth. 'Ten days — no, it's only eight now.'

He groaned. 'We'll make every day count; every minute, every second. I refuse to think about you leaving. What will your parents say?'

'They probably won't be ecstatic about the Canada part of it, but they want me to be happy.'

He hooked a stray strand of hair behind her ear. 'They'll always be welcome, and any other friends or relations.' He pulled her tightly to him. 'How soon can you throw in your job and come back to Pineville?'

Amy caught her breath. 'I'm still in my trial period, so I don't think there'll be much difficulty in breaking my contract. I have other things to cancel, like the flat . . . '

'The last weeks have been hell. I think I'll fly back with you, to meet your parents and help you to wind things up. When you come back you can stay with Ruth again until you're absolutely sure you can commit yourself to sharing my life.' He laughed. 'Oh, Amy! I've dreamed about you for so long, I still can't believe you're here and you're going to be mine. I don't want to share you with anyone else, but there's this party tonight, and I suppose we'll have to have it. Would you like to visit Vancouver again for a couple of days?'

'I'd love to, but know what I'd really like to do?'

'What?'

'To go back to the cabin again.'

'That's a great idea!' He grinned. 'This time we'll take some proper food.' He grew silent as he studied her face. 'Love is the only thing that matters. I'll do all I can to make you happy, Amy.'

'We'll do all we can to make each other happy.'

He held her close. 'I'm looking forward to showing you the best of Canada. Skiing in winter, friendly people, ice hockey — I hope you'll love it. In summer we can go on canoe tours through the wilderness, spend time out at the cabin. Your family will visit us, and we'll visit them. You tell me what you want, and I'll try to make it come true.'

Amy wound her arms round his neck. 'There's only one thing I want; I want you.'

He gave a throaty chuckle and they eyed each other in contentment.

He looked at her wickedly. 'We have eight days now, and the rest of our lives when we've sorted out the other annoying details.

'Then we'll use every second of it from now on.'

Luke nodded and his chuckle turned into laughter. Amy joined in and they were soon oblivious to the flurries that were building drifts of snow against the cabin walls, or of the fluffy flakes grasping at the branches of the rich green firs outside. A covering of sparkling white covered the land and they were unaware of the silence of the hills and mountains around them.

They sat, arms entwined, in front of the fireplace with its crackling logs and listened to the sound of Christmas bells from the church floating up from the little town below. Soon Pineville would be celebrating Christmas, and Amy and Luke knew that this Christmas would be the best one ever.

THE END

We do hope that you have enjoyed reading this large print book.

Did you know that all of our titles are available for purchase?

We publish a wide range of high quality large print books including:
Romances, Mysteries, Classics
General Fiction
Non Fiction and Westerns

Special interest titles available in large print are:
The Little Oxford Dictionary
Music Book, Song Book
Hymn Book, Service Book

Also available from us courtesy of Oxford University Press:
Young Readers' Dictionary
(large print edition)
Young Readers' Thesaurus
(large print edition)

For further information or a free brochure, please contact us at:
Ulverscroft Large Print Books Ltd.,
The Green, Bradgate Road, Anstey,
Leicester, LE7 7FU, England.
Tel: (00 44) 0116 236 4325
Fax: (00 44) 0116 234 0205

WHISPERS ON THE PLAINS

Noelene Jenkinson

Widowed wheat farmer Dusty Nash, of Sunday Plains pastoral station, is captivated by the spirited redhead who arrives in the district. Irish teacher Meghan Dorney has left her floundering engagement for a six-month posting to the outback of Western Australia. Thrown together in the small, isolated community, each resists their budding attraction to resolve personal issues and tragedy. But when Dusty learns the truth about the newcomer, can he forgive enough to love?

SUZI LEARNS TO LOVE AGAIN

Patricia Keyson

Upon meeting troublesome pupil Tom's father, Cameron, young schoolteacher Suzi feels an immediate attraction. She is determined not to be drawn into a relationship, knowing she would feel unfaithful to her late husband; but the more time Cameron and Suzi spend together, the more they are captivated by each other. Suzi rediscovers deep emotions, though she agrees with Cameron that Tom must come first . . . But how long can Suzi hide her love for Cameron?

ED LEISURE + CULTURE